THE CHADWICK CHRONICLES:
VAMPIRE ON THE HIGH SEAS

THE CHADWICK CHRONICLES:

VAMPIRE ON THE HIGH SEAS

JOSEPH SWICK

Matchstick Literary
1-888-306-8885
orders@matchliterary.com

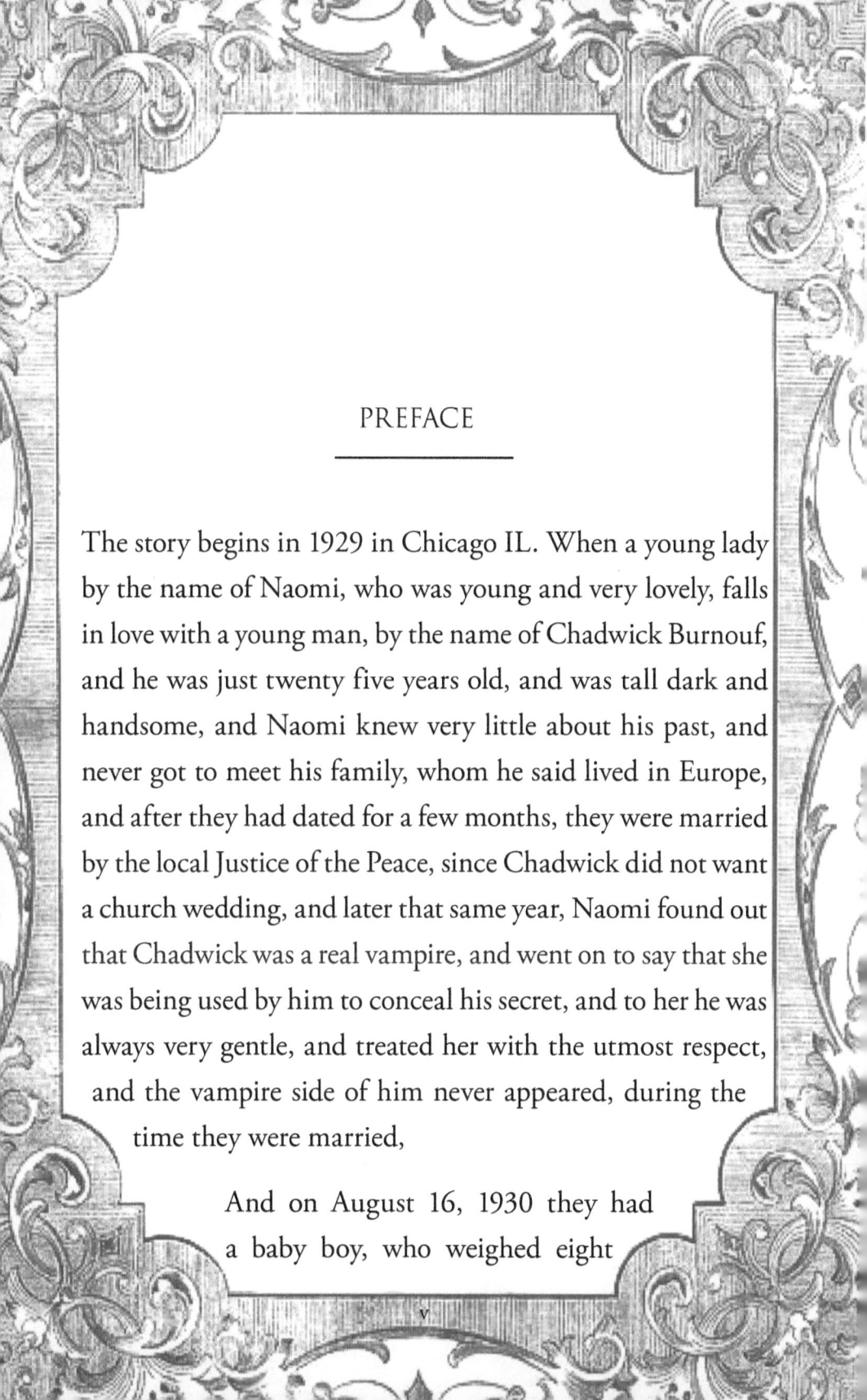

PREFACE

The story begins in 1929 in Chicago IL. When a young lady by the name of Naomi, who was young and very lovely, falls in love with a young man, by the name of Chadwick Burnouf, and he was just twenty five years old, and was tall dark and handsome, and Naomi knew very little about his past, and never got to meet his family, whom he said lived in Europe, and after they had dated for a few months, they were married by the local Justice of the Peace, since Chadwick did not want a church wedding, and later that same year, Naomi found out that Chadwick was a real vampire, and went on to say that she was being used by him to conceal his secret, and to her he was always very gentle, and treated her with the utmost respect, and the vampire side of him never appeared, during the time they were married,

And on August 16, 1930 they had a baby boy, who weighed eight pounds, and three ounces, and he had very pale skin, and jet black hair, and they named him after his father, "Chadwick Burnouf" and also during the year her husband had for the first time confessed, that since he was a vampire, he could not control going out on a hunt, because of his need for blood, and Naomi was too scared to leave the relationship, and even though she knew he was a vampire, down deep in her heart, she knew she still loved him, and just two months after Chadwick Jr. was born, his father Chadwick was killed, while on a hunt, "and after telling Naomi he was going to work," and that night while on a hunt, Chadwick found himself with a pretty young lady who invited him to come inside her apartment, and later he was caught in bed with the young female by her estranged boyfriend, a big wrestler who threw Chadwick into a sharp bedpost which splintered and punctured his heart. Chadwick didn't die right away but was able to leave the ladies residence and went home in a flash, and died in the arms of his wife, and his body turned to ashes very quickly, and Naomi put his ashes into a box and buried them in a nearby cemetery and marked his grave.

So Naomi was left alone to raise her son and as Chadwick Jr. grew up, Naomi sheltered him, and even homeschooled him to keep him away from the public eye as much as possible., "since she knew he might be a vampire", hence to keep him from getting into trouble, but when Chadwick was thirteen, she sat him down and told him the story about his father and about him being a vampire who had a need to hunt ladies in the night, and would suck the blood of females until they were either dead, or turning them into a vampire, and that he had married her to hide his problem, and she also explained that she loved her son very much and wanted all that would be good for him.

She also explained to him as to how his father had died, with a wooden splinter bed post through his heart, while on a hunt, and also, let him know that she was not a vampire, since she was never bitten by Chadwick Sr., and also she explained the only way a vampire could come back to life is for the tears of a sibling or offspring to touch his dead remains.

Chadwick explained to his mother that he often thinks of his dad whom he had never seen, and was glad his mother had shared with him about his father, also Chadwick told his mother that he often had nightmares, and urges to go out at night.

The story begins with Chadwick now twenty five years old, and his struggle to want to live a normal life, and fighting the curse of being a vampire, that is wanting to take over his life, and ever since he was about eighteen years old, he found himself sneaking out of the house, and prowling and hunting on his own.

One day his mother reads in the News Paper about a Medium who will be appearing on the cruise ship, the M.S.S. Goliath, a twenty one day European cruise, and her name was Madam Medina, who is a well-known hypnotist, and somewhat of a good witch, and has also bragged about contacting the unknown, and also helping people who have different types of unusual problems, and Naomi hopes that if Chadwick will make contact with the Madam, while on the cruise ship that he might learn to control the curse of the vampire that is inside him so that he can possibly live a normal life, and Chadwick agrees to go on the cruise, and while on the cruise ship you can feel an unlikely story to unfold, as Chadwick unexpectedly meets a woman who may share his circumstance and this similarity leading to a fateful connection between the two.

CHAPTER
1 – DAY ONE

S eptember 1, 1955 Now in Miami Florida, Chadwick and his Mother Naomi boarded the large Cruise Ship, the M.S.S Goliath, and while Chadwick and his mother were walking to their cabin, at the end of the long hallway, Chadwick noticed a lovely young lady, who was wearing a red and black plaid, knee length skirt, with a six to eight inch split at the bottom, and sported a white blouse that complemented her sexy upper figure, and she was walking up the stairs, and he also noticed her flowing reddish brown hair, and her firm looking calves, and with every step she took, from his view point, he could see some of her smooth looking thigh showing through the split in the skirt, and his heart was throbbing, and he could feel his fangs moving out of his gums, and he wanted to feast on her like a bear eating honey, but for now, he and his mother kept on walking, and he composed himself, and Chadwick and his mother went to their room, number I- 999 on the Imperial Deck, and since it was the first day of the cruise, and Since Chadwick rarely ventured out in the day time, and if he did he almost always wore sunglasses, or a ball cap, or a hat with a brim, or if there was an overcast, hence staying out of the sun as much as possible, so he would sleep most of the day.

And after waking up in the afternoon, on the first day of the voyage, Chadwick and his mother got dressed for dinner, and Chadwick put on his black suit and tie, and his mother put on a flowered dress," and since Chadwick was only half vampire, hopefully no one would be aware of his problem."

After arriving at the main dining room, Chadwick seated his mother, and sat across from her, and after looking at the menu, Chadwick's mother ordered the roast duck, and a baked potato, and a salad, and Chadwick ordered the roast duck as well, and green beans and potatoes.

And when the wine steward came around, Chadwick ordered a bottle of white wine, to be served with dinner, and after toasting to good times on the cruise, and eating a great dinner in the main dining room, Chadwick and his mother went back to their cabin, to room 999 on the Imperial Deck, and to decide what they would be doing for the remainder of the evening, and after sometime of discussing what to do, Chadwick and his mother decided to go to one of the magic shows aboard the big ship, located in the Blue Room, and after walking up two flights of stairs, and arriving at the blue room, Chadwick and his Mother found two empty seats located in the middle of the room, and the show started with the interdiction of Frederick the Magnificent, and the show was great, and as if it was right out of Hollywood or Las Vegas, and the magician first called on a volunteer from the audience, a young blond haired lady with a fair complexion, and she was wearing a knee length skirt that complemented her laced blouse, and she made her way to stage to assist Frederick.

And the magician who was dressed all in black, and was wearing a top hat, ask the young lady to lay down in a box, and not to be afraid, and the box was wooden, and was about four feet long and two feet wide and two feet thick",

and the young lady complied,
and with her feet hanging out of
one end of the box, and her head sticking
out of the other end of the box, the magician
picked up a very large six foot long, toothy steel saw
and began to slowly saw through the wooden box, and also
sawing the young lady in half, and he then moved both pieces
of the sawed box away from each other, while the young lady
was still smiling and moving her feet, and then he pushed the
two pieces of the box back together again, and then opened
the box and the young lady rose up unharmed, and everyone
including Chadwick cheered, and then the magician did some
more illusions,

And then the magician called out from the audience, a
male, about 30 years of age, who had a thin build, and was
wearing a black suit and tie, and had a mustache, and he made
his way to the stage, and the magician ask him to please state
his name, and ask him where was he from, and the man said
his name was Ralph Simson, and that he was from Naples
Florida, and was on the cruise with his family, and then
Frederick asks Ralph to step inside an upright black box,
and he did, and the magician closed the door, and the
box was on casters, so he rolled the box around
so you could see all of the sides, and then
the magician wave a wand, and said

some type of magic words, and then Frederick opened the box, and a dog jumped out, and the man was gone, and the magician then put the dog back into the box and closed the door, and again turned the box three times while saying some magic words, and while waving his wand, and again he opened the door of the box, and the man appeared, and then the magician did a few more magic tricks, and the show closed with all standing and clapping,

And afterwards Chadwick's mother went back to their cabin, and Chadwick went for a stroll around the big ship, the ship was very large, with close to 1500 passengers on board, and over 500 crew members, and it had a small casino, with ten slot machines, and a roulette table, and two poker tables, and shuffleboard on the Lido Deck and two large swimming pools with lots of pool chairs all around the pool area, and at each end of the Lido Deck there was a walk up wet Bar, and just past the Wet Bar was a huge food buffet that stayed open until around eight o'clock at night, and several tables filled the area for passengers to sit at while eating breakfast, lunch or an informal dinner and lots of big windows that overlooked the ocean while dining, and it was a great ship like its namesake, Goliath.

Chadwick then toured the Gym area where they had several exercise types of equipment, and he walked passed a lady who was there using a machine which had a big belt that went around the waist line, and was vibrating, and it was supposed to shake away the pounds while looking at the ocean out of one the big windows, and it was a nice gym for a ship.

After walking to the Bow of the Ship and leaning over the rail, and looking at the moon shining brightly, off of the water as far as he could see, Chadwick began to reminisce about the first time he had the urge to go on a hunt, "knowing that if he was going to come to terms with his problems that he needed to face them head on," Chadwick remembered when he was about eighteen years old, he had sneaked out of his mother's two story house, located at 211 and 54th street in Chicago, Illinois, and he was dressed in all black so he would blend into the darkness, and after walking about three blocks from his residence, Chadwick saw a newly built two story white house, with black shutters and a big picture window in front, and Chadwick noticed a beautiful young girl who looked to be in her twenties who had long brown hair and she was wearing a short pink lace nightgown, while she was walking around in front of the big window, and as he got closer, and closer to the house, while still

looking through the window,
he saw her walking up the steps,
and unknowingly revealing her silk laced
undergarment in every step, and from the outside
of her house he noticed a light come on.

He wanted to get a better look so he climbed a tree outside of her room, and was now looking directly into the young lady's bedroom, and saw her take off her nightgown, and he admired her perfect body, while she was standing there in only her exotic brassiere and raunchy panties, Chadwick noticed a big man who came into her room, and they embraced, "Chadwick was drooling from his mouth like a dog that had contacted rabies, and for the first time his eyes lit amber as they glowed off the ladies window, like a full moon on a clear night, and he noticed for the first time that he had fangs moving in and out of his gums, and he felt them with his tongue "and he wanted the girl all for himself, but there was another man, so he would have to come back another time, when the man was not there..

After Chadwick cased the young lady's residence for about six weeks, Chadwick learned that the man was a truck driver, and was not at home on Fridays and Saturdays every other week, so that's when he would have to make his move.

One Saturday morning at around 2 am, Chadwick remembered sneaking out of their house, and went into their garage, and took a large screw driver from their tool box, and went on the prowl, again wearing all black, his heart was beating insanely fast as he slowly approached the young ladies house and finally he had arrived. He had noticed that the man's truck was not there, and he also noticed a light was on in the upstairs bedroom that he was looking into on prior nights, and he patiently waited for the lights to go out while fantasizing about the ecstasy his first hunt would bring him.

Once the young lady's lights went out, Chadwick slowly walked up to the down stairs window, and forced the window open with his screwdriver, and entered the residence while climbing over the back of a couch in the living room, he then proceeded up the steps, and his heart was racing, and his mouth was wet and he was licking the drool from his lips, his eyes were glowing amber, and his fangs appeared, thinking about the young lady's silky white skin, and her perfect body.

The door was already opened as Chadwick topped the steps, and he stopped at the doorway of the young lady's room, and he watched her while she was lying on the bed, in just her white laced bra and panties, and she then raised up, but to Chadwick's amazement she did not yell out, but instead as if she was hypnotized, or in some type of trance, she raised her right hand and motioned for Chadwick to come closer, and invited him into her room, "Chadwick never knew that he was irresistible to women until that night" and as Chadwick came closer the young lady reached out, and took Chadwick by the hand and pulled him onto her bed, and he started kissing her and caressing her plump breast under her laced bra, while she was moaning, and said for him not to stop, and he then moved his other hand down, and put it inside of the lady's panties, while touching her moist skin, as she opened her legs, he entered her body with his finger and he could feel her throbbing, while he moved it back and forth, feeling her wetness, and she begged him to make love to her, as she reached down and unzipped Chadwick's pants, and pulled out his erect manhood, and pulled it toward her wanting body, and as he penetrated her tight wet body, she screamed with pleasure, as Chadwick moved back and forth, and hearing her panting, and groaning for more, and he reached around with his right hand and squeezed her ass, as he excelled and exploded deep inside the young lady, and she screamed loud, in pleasure, and then after losing all of his control, Chadwick's fangs appeared again, and with his mouth wide open while holding the lady's arms to her side, he made contact with her skin, as his fangs entered the young lady's neck fresh blood was oozing from the opened wound, Chadwick could hear the young lady screaming in brutal pain, and he began sucking on her blood until he was completely satisfied, and then after finishing his meal he left the body of the woman who one could not even recognize any more on the bed and left in shame as he had completed his first hunt.

And the next day Chadwick cried after reading the local newspaper head line, *"Murder between 211th & 54th street"*

And the fight began for Chadwick to try and control the ragging curse of the vampire that was inside of him, and to one day become a normal person, and not a murdering freak of nature.

And then Chadwick remembered another time on a hunt while he and his mother was in Georgia to attend her best friend's Wedding, at the reception in the large community building, Chadwick wandered down the stairs, and was walking down the long hallway, and Chadwick saw a young lady who looked to be 18 or 19 years old and was wearing a pink dress, and noticed her long brown hair, that was very

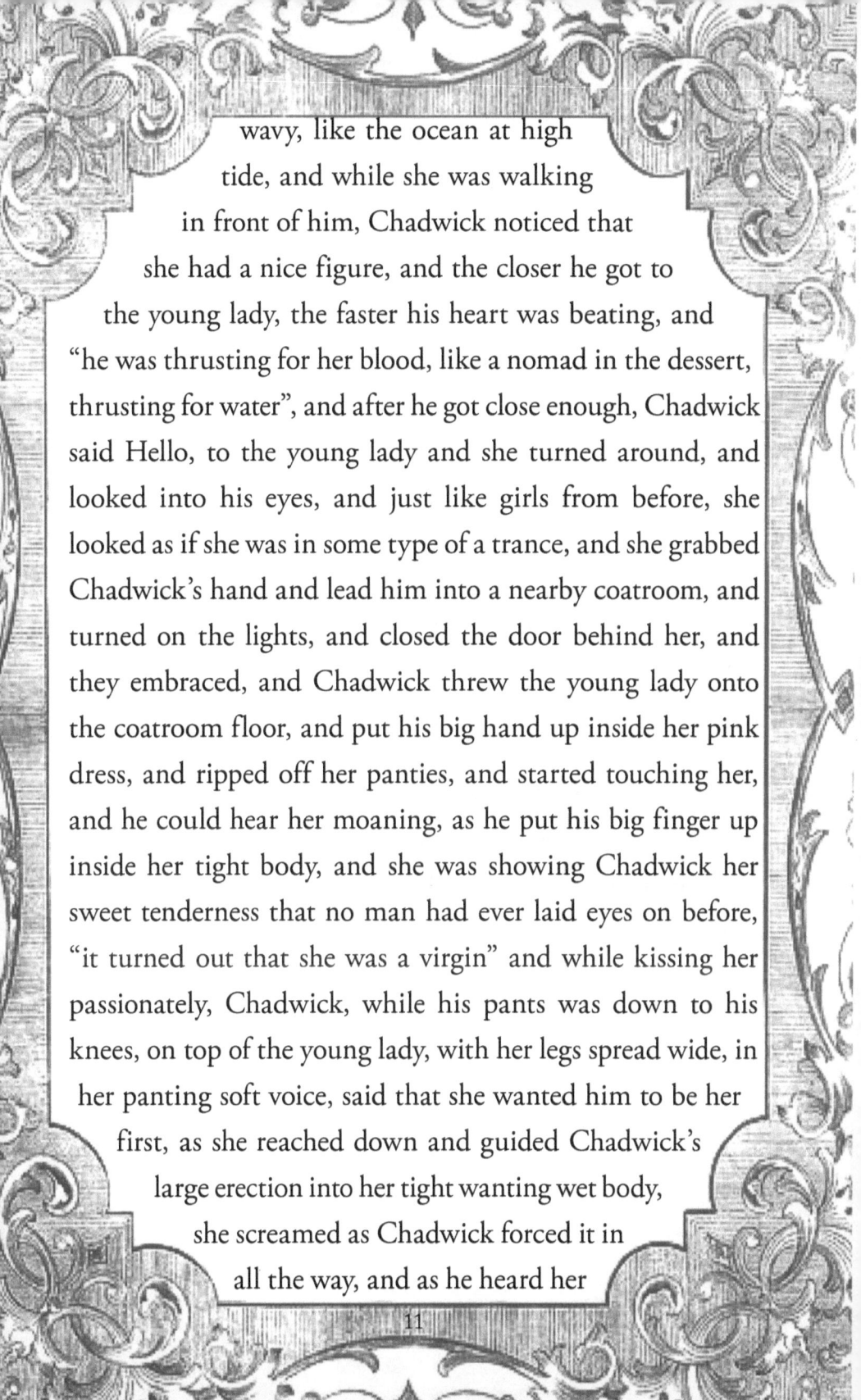

wavy, like the ocean at high tide, and while she was walking in front of him, Chadwick noticed that she had a nice figure, and the closer he got to the young lady, the faster his heart was beating, and "he was thrusting for her blood, like a nomad in the dessert, thrusting for water", and after he got close enough, Chadwick said Hello, to the young lady and she turned around, and looked into his eyes, and just like girls from before, she looked as if she was in some type of a trance, and she grabbed Chadwick's hand and lead him into a nearby coatroom, and turned on the lights, and closed the door behind her, and they embraced, and Chadwick threw the young lady onto the coatroom floor, and put his big hand up inside her pink dress, and ripped off her panties, and started touching her, and he could hear her moaning, as he put his big finger up inside her tight body, and she was showing Chadwick her sweet tenderness that no man had ever laid eyes on before, "it turned out that she was a virgin" and while kissing her passionately, Chadwick, while his pants was down to his knees, on top of the young lady, with her legs spread wide, in her panting soft voice, said that she wanted him to be her first, as she reached down and guided Chadwick's large erection into her tight wanting wet body, she screamed as Chadwick forced it in all the way, and as he heard her

yell, it hurts, but don't stop,
he could smell the fresh virgin
blood, and wanted a taste, and she kept
on panting loudly, with every motion, and
saying please don't stop, and Chadwick exploded deep
inside her tight young body, and she screamed, in pain and
pleasure, and Chadwick could still smell the blood from the
young virgin, and then his heart started beating faster, and
his eyes lit amber, and his fangs came out, and he bit into her
tender neck, while putting her scarf in her mouth to keep her
from screaming anymore, and he then sucked all of the life
out of the young lady until he was completely satisfied, and
he left her partly nude body lying on the coat room floor, and
later felt bad for what he had done.

After he stopped remembering, Chadwick found himself
with his back to the rails of the cruise ship, and he was crying
and then he went back to cabin I-999 on the imperial Deck
where his mother was waiting.

CHAPTER -2-

September 2, 1955, Chadwick slept all day after being up most of the night. And at around 4pm... His mother had woken him up and explained that Madam Medina was going to be in the green room tonight at eight o'clock, and she would be doing a two hour show, and said they should go see her show, and try to make contact with her, and make an appointment to see her about Chadwick's problem.

Chadwick agreed and so after getting dressed, Chadwick and his mother left their cabin, and started walking up to the main dining room, located on the

Promenade Deck of the big ship, and the formal dining room was beautifully lit with candles all around, and with white linen table cloths, and chandeliers hanging from the ceiling, and it was like a picturesque scenery and Chadwick seated his mother and found that they were seated across from a young lady, and her mother who was from Austin, Texas. The young lady was very lovely, and Chadwick spoke to her, and she said her name was Tracy Fields while beaming a smile, and she went on to say that she was attending college, and was studying to be a nurse back in Austin. Tracy had long brown hair, blue eyes and a great complexion as well as a perfect figure, and looked as if she worked out a lot.

And Tracy explained that maybe they could see some of the ship together later on, since she was single as well, and Chadwick told Tracy that maybe they could get together later, because he and his mother were going to the Madam Medina show after dinner.

After eating Chadwick and his mother left the dining room. Afterwards they walked around for a while admiring the vastness of the ship, and commented as to how beautiful it was, and they stopped by one of the four bars, and had a drink and talked.

Then at 10 minutes before eight o'clock, Chadwick and his mother left the bar, and went into the green room to see The Madam Medina Show, and once they arrived they found that it was very crowded, and that they had to sit all the way at the back of the room and once they were seated, one of the crew members, introduced Madam Medina, a lady in her early fifties, wearing all black, with jet black hair, and had a pale complexion. She came out from behind the curtain and onto the stage floor and sat down at a table in the middle of the stage floor, and she said in a gruff voice "Good Evening and welcome everyone."

Covering the table was a black tablecloth, and what appeared to be a box about the size of a shoe box in the center of the table facing her, and 2 chairs, one where she was sitting and one across from her.

Madam Medina went into what appeared to be a trance, and was slowly waving her hands over the black box and she started chanting then prophetically she called out a man from the audience, and invited him to sit across from her at the table, and once on stage the man sat across from the Madam, and she began telling him he was a chain smoker, and ask if he was trying to quit.

And the man explained that the Madam was right, and he was a chain smoker and had been trying to quit for some time, and so far, he was unable to quit and did not have the willpower, and hopes she can help him.

The Madam looked deeply into the man's eyes and as the man looked back deeply into her eyes, he went into a trance and she said in her gruffly voice, She uttered some type of incantation and then said smoking is bad for you and very unhealthy so from now on if you even hear someone offering you a cigarette, you will feel sick to your stomach, and from this day forward you will not be able to be in the same room with a smoker again, and she chanted very loudly, while still waving her hands in front of the man's face, and then she snapped her fingers, and the man opened his eyes, and looked all around the room with his eyes opened widely, and he looked like a deer with a light shining it its eyes at night, and then Madam Medina ask the young man" would you like a cigarette sir"? And the young man said no and grabbed his stomach and ran off of the stage.

Madam Medina while sitting at the table was waving her hands over the black box and chanting and she prophetically in her loud gruffly voice called out a thirty-year-old woman, with long brown hair tied back with a blue and white bow and wearing a blue jumper. The Madam invited her to sit at her table, and the lady made her way up to the stage and sat at the table, and Madam Medina advised the female that she saw in her mind's eye that she had been in deep depression and was threading suicide from time to time, and could not control her depression even with drugs, and went on to say that her self-esteem was very low. The female was amazed that Madam Medina knew all of that information, and agreed to what she had said. Again, Madam Medina advised the young lady to look into her eyes and so the lady did and then the young lady also went into a trance and Madam Medina started to chant again in a language that none of them had ever heard before and then Madam Medina said while looking into the black box and waving her hands in front of lady "from this day forward you will have high self-esteem and you will love yourself again and you will think only good thoughts from now on" After chanting very loudly and saying some kind of incantation, and while waving her hands in front the lady's face, Madam Medina snapped her fingers, and the young lady looked all around with a surprised look on her face, and

Madam Medina asked "How do you feel?" and she jumped up and laughed and said that she felt like she was on top of the world and she shook hands with Madam Medina and thanked her and left the stage in great spirits.

And while the Madam was waving her hands over the black box in the middle of the table, red smoke came out of the box, as she called out another person from the audience to join her, on the stage, and it was an elderly lady who looked to be in her late 60's, and she had her gray hair in a bun, and she was wearing a flowered long dress, and she was walking with a cane, and when the lady made it up to the stage, Madam Medina asked her to sit down across from her, and the lady sat down and Madam Medina told the lady that she feels that she had lost someone close to her in the last month, and thinks it was either a brother or a cousin, who was very close to her, and that he had been missing, and it was not known if he was alive or dead, the lady agreed and said that her brother, Charley, had walked away from the convalescence home where he was staying about a month ago and was not seen or heard from, and Madam Medina told the lady to look deeply into her eyes, and the lady did, and also went into some type of a trance, and Madam Medina again waived her hands over the black box in the middle of the table, and red smoke arose from the box as Madam Medina told the lady that she has made contact with her brother Charley from the beyond, and Charley wants her to know that on the night that he left the home, he fell down a hill about a half a mile from home, and rolled into a raging river and drowned in that area, and most likely his body would never be found, and Madam Medina said that Charley wants everyone to know that he has always loved all of his family, and to tell you not to worry, and that he is now in a place where he does not have to suffer anymore, and for you to go on with your life, and live it to the fullest, and then the Madam started chanting loudly, as more smoke appeared from the box and Madam Medina snapped her fingers, and the lady's eyes opened, and looked amazed, and she had a big smile on her face, and told Madam Madina, that she knows that she was telling the truth, and had been in contact with her brother, because there is a big rapid flowing river about a half a mile from their home where he had been staying and the lady thanked Madam Medina and shook her hand and then left the stage with a big smile on her face.

Chadwick and his mother was impressed with Madam Medina, but that night they never made it backstage to speak

with her, and had to wait for
another time so Chadwick and
his mother left the area and stopped
by one of the coffee shops, and had coffee
and donuts and talked for a while about Chadwick's
problems and hoped that Madam Medina could help him..

Meanwhile Chadwick's mother started to head back to the imperial deck near their room after Chadwick advised her, he was going to walk around the ship for a while his mother said that would be fine but to be careful.

And after walking around for a while, Chadwick again found himself standing at the bow of the ship, and while looking at the white caps on the water as far as he could see, on this cloudy night, and again remembering about another time when he was on a hunt, when he was just eighteen years old, it was about six months after his first hunt, he and his mother had went on vacation to the Virginia beach for a week and they were staying at a nice beach front hotel, and on the second day of their trip, while he and his mother was walking to their hotel room, Chadwick noticed a young lady who looked to be in her late twenties and she was kissing either her boyfriend or husband at the door of her hotel room, just three doors down from their room, and while Chadwick was taking his time opening their hotel door to their room and it was around 11 pm when Chadwick overheard the beautiful young lady telling her man, not to be out too late, and the young man explained that he was going to be visiting a friend whom he had not seen in a while, who was staying at another hotel and that he would be gone for about three hours.

Chadwick proceeded into he and his mother's room, and once inside their room the more Chadwick thought about the young lady just three doors down, the more he wanted her, thinking of her tan long legs and how nice she looked in her short blue skirt, and her long flowing blonde hair, and then Chadwick decided to make his move and he told his mother he was going to go out for a walk, on this hot summer night, and would be back in a while, and then he left, and walked to the young ladies room and knocked on the door, and she came to the door wearing only a mans checkered shirt, showing off her long tan legs, and almost like she was in a trance or hypnotized, Chadwick noticed her eyes were wide open, and she invited him into her room, and she started kissing him and pulling him closer to her lovely flawless tan body, and she unbuttoned Chadwick's shirt and started rubbing her soft hands over his bare chest, while helping him unzip his pants, and he was caressing her beautiful body as he put his right hand on her smooth rounded ass, as they both fell on the bed while still holding each other, and she grabbed Chadwick's large erection and put the tip into her mouth, and he could feel her hot breath, and her tongue, then she took it out of her wet mouth, and laying down she, pulled him inside of her while moaning and groaning, and she panted heavily, as Chadwick was moving in and out of her tight body, and he was kissing her neck and he grabbed and squeezed her ass with passion, and pleasure as he could not hold out any longer and he injected her sweaty tight body with everything he had, and she screamed with pleasure, as they both were in there own little utopia, and then like before Chadwick's eyes lite amber, and he started drooling at the mouth, and his fangs moving out of his gums, and like a tiger biting into a rabbit his fangs entered the young ladies neck, and blood squirted all over, as she screamed out, almost with pleasure as Chadwick sucked the life out of the young lady, and left her room in a flash, and went back to he and his mother's room, and again the next day Chadwick cried, and felt bad for what he had done and knowing deep inside that he wanted to live a normal life and to be able to control the rage that was inside of him.

Then Chadwick started to remember a time when he and his mother were traveling across country on a passenger train, and it was a three day train ride so they each had their own sleeping quarters, Chadwick's Mom had an upper berth bunk and Chadwick had the lower, and on the second day of the trip while in the dining compartment Chadwick saw a fairly good looking plainly dressed young lady, who made eye contact with him from across the room while he was eating and she was also smiling every time he would look at her and he later followed her to her bunk area and saw where she was rooming and at around twelve o'clock that night he found himself on the prowl, and just outside the lady's compartment, he found himself sweating and to his amazement the young lady whom had smiled at him, while eating dinner earlier, came walking out of her compartment, and this time while smiling told Chadwick that her name was Tammy Johnson and that she and her family were going to be visiting friends who lives in Indiana and after Chadwick introduced himself, he proceeded to tell Tammy that he and his mother was on vacation taking a train trip across the County. After conversing for a while Tammy asked Chadwick if he wanted to go to the outside car so they could look at the stars and Chadwick agreed and they walked to the back of the train and outside while admiring the stars and looking at the lights of the houses. Tammy put her arms around Chadwick and started kissing him, and told Chadwick that she wanted him to make love to her, and that she had not been with a man for about six months and after they embraced, Chadwick, while kissing Tammy, put his big hand down into Tammy's pajamas, and started rubbing the wet hair between her legs, as Tammy moaned and groaned loudly she pulled down her pajama bottoms that was under her flannel night shirt, and she bent over the rail of the outside car, holding on with both hands while showing Chadwick her bare naked rear end and she moaned and said come on take me, as Chadwick unzipped his pants, and splitting her cheeks with his large erection he penetrated her soft body and in a ramming sensation he moved forward, entering deep inside her and as he slapped her hard on the ass, and she yelled out saying, that it hurts, and that he is so big inside her, and was screaming, but Chadwick just kept on going for about twenty minutes, until he climaxed at the same time hearing her scream in pleasure, while the train whistled for a crossing and Chadwick's heart was beating faster and faster and he felt his fangs moving out of his gums, and his eyes lit bright amber and the young lady screamed as he penetrated her soft neck, and blood shot into the

night air as he drained the life
out of the young female and let
her fall off of the train near a farm house
about fifty miles out of Indiana and he jerked
his head back and stopped remembering his past while
hanging over the rail of the ship and still at the bow.

He heard a voice call out "Chadwick! Chadwick!" calling his name, and it was Tracy. Chadwick spoke to her and said that he had just been enjoying the night air, coming off of the ocean, and she said that she just thought she would go out for a stroll around the ship, and ended up here at the bow, and Chadwick and Tracy walked around together for a while, getting to know each other a little better, and Tracy explained that she had wanted to be a nurse one day and liked the idea of helping people, and Chadwick explained that his dad died when his was a baby, and left him and his mother a lot of money, so he did not ever have to work unless he wanted, but he was an inspiring author and had been working on a playwright for a possible movie and Tracy was impressed so Tracy explained that there was a cocktail party onboard the ship tomorrow night and would like him to escort her and told him that it was in the black tie room on the Verandah deck at 10 pm and Chadwick said that it sounded like a lot of fun, and thanked her for asking him, and while Chadwick was walking with Tracy back to her room, he couldn't help but notice her sweet smelling perfume, her soft hands and her lovely smile, and after arriving at Tracy's door, Chadwick kissed her on the cheek and told her he had fun walking with her, and that he would love to see her tomorrow, and then Chadwick went back to the imperial deck to he and his mother's cabin.

Tracy while in her room, got dressed for bed and laid down, and was thinking about the new person in her life, and as to how nice of a person he was, but she also knew that she had some problems, that she could not tell Chadwick at least not just yet because her problems were deep within, and sometimes kept her from sleeping or being able to live a normal life but would Chadwick understand, if she told him, and after reasoning and going back and forth in her mind, she decide not to tell him for now, but maybe after she gets to know him better she would tell him, and then she closed her eyes and went to sleep.

CHAPTER
3 DAY THREE

On September 3, 1955, after porting in Nassau, Bahamas' and at around noon, Chadwick's mom wakes him, and they talk about his night with Tracy, and she asks Chadwick about all of the things that they had done while walking around, and Chadwick told her and explained that he thinks he was falling in love with Tracy and his mother said that she was very glad for him, but sounded a bit cautious due to the tone of her voice, and Chadwick explained that Tracy wanted him to escort her to the cocktail party tonight, and that he would be spending the evening with her, and his mother said that it sounded like a great idea and she would find something to do on the vast ship, and he and his mother decided they would go onto the Island today and go sightseeing and then spend some time on the beach, and Chadwick put on his light colored shorts and a polo shirt, and his mother put on her daisy flowered print dress, and a white hat, and then they walked up to the main dining room to eat lunch.

And after seating his mother at the dining table, Chadwick sat across from her, and ordered sweet potatoes, baked ham, coffee and water while his mother had baked potato, a salad and a coffee. They talked about what a great time they were having so far on the Cruise ship, and after lunch, Chadwick put on his sunglasses before leaving the ship, and he and his mother walked off of the ship onto the gangway and went to the Island.

Chadwick was amazed at how blue and clear the water was in the Bahamas' as if a deity had made sure to make the water look majestic so he and his mother admired the beauty of the palm trees, the climate and started taking pictures right away, as they walked toward the town, and the first thing they decided was to take a tour of the Island so they took a horse carriage ride through the Island,

and once on the carriage the
man at the reins was giving them
a history lesson during the ride, and it
was an amazing learning experience about the
founder of the Island while hearing the clipping of
the horses hooves on the cobblestone streets and hearing the
carriage driver explain how the Island got to be a main tourist
attraction in the Bahamas and pointing out their Capitol
Building and State flower.

The carriage ride lasted for about one hour and then
Chadwick and his mother got a rum drink from one of the
thatched roof, type of Palm leaf covered bars and then they
continued to walk to the beach, after walking for a while they
arrived at the beach, and they sat down at one of the thatched
roof tables and finished their tall rum drink while admiring
the beauty that was in front of them and the sand was like
white powdered sugar and the clear blue water glistened in
the sun light and Chadwick went wading with his shoes off
and pants rolled up. The sand felt cool between his toes, and
the water was great, while he was thinking about the pretty
young lady that he was falling in love with, and wished that
she was there to spend each moment with him.

After a few hours at the beach Chadwick
and his mother went back to the ship,
and his mother explained that

she had a ball on the Island, and relaxing on the beach, and said she hoped after tomorrow night's show featuring Madam Medina, that they might be able to meet with her about Chadwick's problems, and hope she would be able to help him, and then Chadwick and his mother went back to their cabin to rest up for tonight.

At four thirty P.M., Chadwick and his mother began getting ready for the big night on the ship, and his mother put on a beautiful red gown, and stiletto heels, and a pearl necklace that complemented her beauty, and then put her hair in a bun on top of her head, and Chadwick put on a white tuxedo with tails, and a white shirt with a red bow tie and cumberbun, and black polished shoes because "after all he was going to a formal cocktail party with a beautiful young lady", and at around six P.M. Chadwick and his mother went to dinner in the main dining room, and every man was dressed in their tuxedos, and the ladies all in their gowns, and it looked fit for a prince, "and Chadwick felt like a king", and Tracy and her mother came in to the dining room and Tracy looked gorgeous, in a stunning style rose colored gown that hugged her beautiful body, and was wearing a diamond accented choker and eyes that reflected the light from the room,

and her face glowed like a
new moon on a clear night and
she stared into Chadwick's eyes, and
beholding a smile that would bring any man to
his knees, "and Chadwick, being a gentleman" seated
Tracy and her mother at the table, and her mother said "you
kids have fun tonight at the party, and laughingly said, "but
not too much fun haha!"

After a gourmet dinner with red wine, Chadwick and
Tracy excused themselves, and advised their mothers that
they were going to walk around the big ship for a while and
then later, they would be going to the cocktail party. Tracy
and Chadwick first walked out onto the Lido Deck and then
went to a more secluded area that was on the next deck up,
and while they were all alone embracing each other while
listening to the waves hitting the sides of the ship, they gazed
at the white caps on the water as far as one could see.

Tracy told Chadwick she liked him a lot, and pulled him
closer, and as they made eye contact and there lips touched,
and they kissed and talked about how nice it was being
together, and after about half an hour, Chadwick explained
that they should be going because it was about time
for the cocktail party to start, and they left arm
in arm, and as they entered the party,
there was a big band playing, and

the lights were dim, and some
of the people were mingling, and
others were dancing to the waltz.

Chadwick asked Tracy if she wanted to dance
and she smilingly said of course, and took Chadwick's
hand and as they danced closely, Chadwick was thinking how
nice it was and how sweet smelling Tracy's perfume was and
she put her head on his shoulder, and he now knew he had
feelings for Tracy, that he had never experienced before, but
Chadwick also knew in the back of his mind, the secret that
he could never reveal because she or any other lady would not
understand, and he knew now more than ever that he had
to make contact with Madam Medina to try and become a
normal person so he could further his relationship with Tracy.

After the dance Chadwick, and Tracy found a table, and
ordered cocktails, and Tracy talked about her future as a
nurse, and how she one day would like to marry, and have kids
and Chadwick also talked about his future as a playwright
and said he also someday would like to get married, and that
he wanted kids as well and that he was just waiting for the
right woman to come into his life and after another drink,
Tracy put out her right hand and smiled and ask if
Chadwick would like to dance again, and he
said "I would love to" and they went
onto the dance floor and Tracy

pulled Chadwick very close
to her body, and he could feel her
plump breast close to his body. And he
loved the smell of her sweet perfume as she put
her head on his shoulder, and he whispered into her
ear and told her how nice she smelled.

And after dancing for a while they went back to their table, and Tracy asked Chadwick about his father, and Chadwick explained that his father was in the Navy and was gone a lot, and had come from a wealthy family in Europe, and that he had died at sea when Chadwick was just a baby and that his remains were sent back to Chicago where he was buried and so he never knew his father, and Tracy explained that they have something else in common, because her dad had also died when she was a baby after an auto accident while going to work. After a night of dancing and toasting to a wonderful night, Tracy ask Chadwick if he wanted to go back to the deck where they were earlier, to spend some time alone, and Chadwick said that sounded great, and they both left arm in arm smiling and chit-chatting, as they walked toward the deck.

Once they arrived at the smokestack deck, they
found that they were all alone and Tracy put
her arms around Chadwick's neck, and
pulled him close to her body,

and he could feel the warmth
of her body close to his, and was
very excited, and they began kissing
and enjoying the taste and smell of each other,
and after about an hour at around one A.M., Tracy
said they had better be getting back to their rooms, and
Chadwick reluctantly said yes, and walked her back to her
room and they embraced after arriving at her door and said
their good nights, and Chadwick left and walked up to the
lido deck and to the bow of the ship, and while leaning over
the rail and looking out at the darkness on the water,

Chadwick remembered one night in Chicago, while he
was out walking around, he came upon a late night bar and
went inside and he sat down on a bar stool and ordered a beer,
and a lady who appeared to be in her upper 20's came up to
him, and she was very pretty and had a great figure and was
wearing a white skirt, knee length with a split, showing off
some of her bare thigh, and it hugged her body like a glove,
and she was drunk, and wanted him to walk her home, and
she told Chadwick that she lived in an apartment near the
bar, and after finishing his beer Chadwick advised her he
would walk her home, and after helping her put on
her coat Chadwick walked the young lady to her
apartment building, which was located a
few blocks away, and after arriving,

the young lady invited him in, and as he entered the young ladies apartment, he noticed that it smelled of cigarette smoke, and overall it was very messy and dark, and the young lady fell onto the couch with her legs into the air showing her entire naked body, and she gasped and said "take me Chadwick!" and Chadwick undid his pants and took off his shirt and jumped on her, and pulled off her undergarments and pulled off her top revealing her very large breast and like a mad man out of an asylum, he made love to her for about fifteen to twenty minutes, hearing her groaning and panting in pleasure, and then his eyes lit amber and his fangs appeared, and entered her tiny neck, and blood was squirting and she screamed very loud, and Chadwick sadly remembered sucking all the life out of young lady and left her residence in a flash, and went home.

And again, the next day he felt really bad for what he had done, and prayed, that if there is a God to please forgive him.

One other time Chadwick remembered that when he and his mother were on vacation, just off of the coast of North Carolina, Chadwick had met a young lady, by the name of Nancy who was an accountant and lived and worked in the local area. She was in her thirties, very good looking and after a couple of dates, she asked him if

he wanted to go sailing with
her, and Chadwick told her he
had never tried sailing, but thinks it
might be fun, and she told him that she goes
out to sea alone sailing, several times a year and loves
the ocean, and that she was raised around boats and so
Chadwick agreed to go sailing with her

And the next day Chadwick and Nancy went onto her
boat, and she guided him as to what to do on the boat, and
once out at sea, and just off of the coast, Chadwick could not
help but notice the ladies long tan legs, when she removed her
cut off blue jean shorts, that complimented her white bathing
suit underneath and once they past the break water, Nancy
had Chadwick pull down the mask, and they went into the
bottom of the sailboat and then Nancy opened a bottle of red
wine, and poured two glasses, and sat down beside Chadwick
and they started kissing and caressing each other while still
sipping their wine and Nancy while dropping her wine glass
laid down onto the floor of the boat, and pulled Chadwick on
top of her and said she wanted to feel him inside of her and
they made love for about an hour, and after reaching a climax
like an erupting volcano, Nancy screamed and moaned
with pleasure, and Chadwick felt his fangs
coming out as his heart was beating fast,
and as his eyes turned into amber,

he started to enter the ladies
neck with his fangs, they heard a
fog horn blowing above deck, and they
both dressed fast and ran out to see what it was,
and it was a Coast Guard cutter boat and after coming
closer to their boat, they advised they were checking all boats
for smugglers, and wanted to come aboard and Nancy who
had her proper papers invited them aboard, and after about
half an hour of checking all over there boat, the Coast Guard
left the area and so did Chadwick and Nancy.

And then Chadwick came out of his trance of the past,
and found himself crying over the railing of the big ship and
said "I've got to get this under control" and then he walked
back to his cabin.

CHAPTER
4/DAY FOUR

September 4, 1955, Now after leaving the islands and now on the high seas, Chadwick awakes after sleeping most of the day, the seas are turbulent and agitated. Chadwick was feeling a little seasick, and he ask the steward to bring him some ginger root to their room,"knowing that ginger is a natural cure for seasickness" and after the cabin steward brought Chadwick some ginger, he made a drink out of it by putting it into a glass of water and adding a little sugar and then after consuming the ginger drink, in about an hour he was feeling better. He and his mother got dressed and went to dinner and like before

Chadwick seated his mother, and then Tracy and her mother came into the dining room and Tracy was more beautiful than ever, wearing a blue plaid knee length skirt, showing off her full smooth caves and perfect body. She also sported a white ruffled blouse that conformed to her gorgeous upper figure. Chadwick seated both of them and Tracy's mother asked Chadwick if he and Tracy had a nice time at the cocktail party last night and Chadwick explained that he and Tracy had a great time, dancing, walking around the big ship and Tracy concurred and went on to explain that she didn't know when she would had a better time ever, and after talking and eating.

Chadwick asked Tracy if she wanted to meet him later on the smokestack deck, "the Deck above the Lido deck" because he and his mother was going to the Madam Medina show in the green room after dinner and told her that the show starts at eight o'clock and maybe they could meet at around eleven o'clock at the smokestack deck and Tracy agreed to meet him there.

After dinner, Chadwick and his mother went their separate ways and on the way to the show, Chadwick and his mother stopped by one of the bars to get a rum and cola, and his mother also lit up a cigarette, and explained that she hoped that Chadwick would get to meet with the Madam tonight and would be able to try and solve his problem and she asked Chadwick if he had any problems with the curse since they had come aboard the ship and Chadwick explained that he had some urges but so far was able to control himself and thinking of Tracy was a big help, and that he is trying to control the rage when it presents itself and went on to say that he hopes that Madam Medina can help him because he now wants to live a normal life more than ever.

At 7:45 P.M. Chadwick and his mother left the bar and headed toward the green room, and after entering the room, they found as before that it was very crowded, but they were able to find a seat near the back of the room and like before on the stage was a rectangular table covered with a black tablecloth and there was a black box about the size of a shoe box sitting in the middle of the table and the Madam was brought onto the stage after a brief introduction, by one of the crew members and it was very dark in the room and the Madam came out and sat down at the table and said with her gruffly voice, "good evening everyone and welcome to my world" She started to wave her hands, palms down and crossing them over the black box and said she could see in her mind's eye that there was a female in the audience who was having problems with her legs and that she could barely walk without assistance and about three rows back a man stood up beside a lady who had a cane by her side and said this is the lady pointing downward to the lady so the Madam motioned for them to come up to the stage and the man helped the lady who appeared to be in her thirties onto the stage and Madam Medina advised her to sit down across from her at the table and the lady did. The Madam advised the man to leave the stage and so the man walked away and the Madam asked the young lady about her condition, and how she got that way, and the lady explained that she was playing polo on one of their estates and a horse threw her off, and she had injured her spine. It was causing her not to be able to walk without assistance and the Madam then waved her hands over the black box and looked deeply into the ladies eyes, and again as if both were in some type of a trance, the Madam told the lady that she would be walking off the stage without assistance, as she yelled out some type of incantation, and shouted out and said "you will walk again" and blue smoke came out of the box, and the lights all went out in the green room for about ten seconds, and came back on, and you could hear the audience gasp because when the lights came back on

the lady was standing in front
of the Madam, and the Madam
said to the lady "throw down that cane
and leave the stage" and the lady while smiling
threw away the cane and jumped off of the stage and
ran toward her man, laughing and crying in happiness, and
the people came to their feet and was clapping in awe.

And then the Madam said "while waving her hands over
the black box, and in her raspy voice "There is a troubled
man of alcohol in the midst of the crowd" and he wants to be
helped yet he has nowhere to turn and the Madam said she
believes that he is in his fifties, and a man who looked to be
in his fifties, who had partly gray hair, and wearing a brown
suit with an open collar shirt, stood up in row five, and said
"I think you mean me" The Madam said for him to come
on up, and the man made his way to the stage, and told the
Madam after sitting across from her at the table, that he has
tried everything to give up drinking, and has been trying to
quit for years and said that he had been an alcoholic ever since
his wife had died with cancer about eight years ago. He was
trying to hold back his tears as he recalled his past, he told
the Madam that he was very lonely, and this was the first
time that he had ventured out, since his wife had
died and said that he had thought about
killing himself from time to time,

but could not, and said that
he found that the answer to his
problems was in a whiskey bottle, and
that he often went to sleep and woke up drunk,
and the man went on to say that he and his wife had
one child, whom had died in a vehicle accident, about two
years before his wife who was diagnosed with cancer and he
went on to say that he was a wealthy man, but was an unhappy
wealthy man, who was nothing more than a worthless drunk
and the Madam told the man to look deep into her eyes, and
the man did, and she was waving her hands over the black
box, in the middle of the table, and started to chant loudly,
and green smoke came from the box, and she told the man,
that he was a good man deep inside, and that his good side
needed to supersede his bad side, and then she yelled out
some type on an incantation afterwards the Madam stood
up waving her hands and said, "from here on out you will
not be able to stay around when anyone is drinking alcohol,
and from here on out if someone offers you a drink, it will
be the same as them offering you your worst tasting food or
poison, and from this day forward you will love yourself, and
have greater self-esteem, and self-worth" and the Madam
went on to say that his wife and daughter would
have wanted him to live a full, and happy
life, and then the Madam Snapped
her fingers loudly, and the man

opened his bulging eyes and Madam Medina asked the man, "would you like some rum sir?" and the man stood up, and said "Hell no!" and had a big smile on his face and said that he was headed to the coffee shopped and hoped that he will possibly meet someone there and he thanked the Madam and left the stage.

At this time Chadwick's mother looked at Chadwick, and said that if Madam Medina can help those people then she can help anyone and after the show ended, Chadwick and his mother walked toward the stage, and hoped that they might meet with the Madam in private, and so they walked backstage and found a door partly opened so Chadwick knocked on the door and to their disbelief there was Madam Medina, who was sitting on a couch, and in a growling voice she said "come on in, and how may I be of help to you?" Chadwick and his mother entered into the Madam's room and the Madam said "please close the door behind you." Chadwick's mother closed the door and after sitting down for a while, Chadwick and his mother started explaining to the Madam about Chadwick's problems, and telling her that Chadwick's father was a full-fledged vampire and how he had died when Chadwick was a baby and that she was not a vampire and that Chadwick was somewhere in between and wanted to live a normal life, and wanted to get rid of the curse of being a vampire and went on to say that she had sheltered Chadwick from the public eye most of his life.

After hearing their story Madame Medina comes to a decision.

She decides to try to help Chadwick, but tells him that this is a bigger problem and will take more than just one or two sessions and that he must fully believe in her ways and not to doubt her in any way, and that it may take several sessions before breaking the curse of the vampire, but she believes she can help him and if Chadwick is willing to do his part and so Chadwick agrees and she sets up a date when she does not have a show to begin helping Chadwick and the Madam opened up a date book and said that the first date open would be on September 6th at 8 o'clock in the evening at her cabin. Chadwick and his mother agree on the time and date and they leave Madam's room to walk around the big ship. Chadwick's mother went back to their cabin to room I-999, after he told her that he was going to be meeting with Tracy, and Chadwick walked up to the Smokestack deck to wait for Tracy, and while leaning over the ship's railing, and watching the ocean, Chadwick started thinking about how much that he cares for Tracy, and knowing that he has to beat

the curse that is wanting
to take over his life, before he
could live a normal life, and then he
heard someone walking up the steps, and he
turned around and it was Tracy, she looked lovely as
she walked over to where he was standing, with his back
against the rails. Chadwick said that he had been waiting for
her and was thinking about the great times that they have
had together while on the cruise, and Tracy agreed and she
said that she had missed Chadwick very much, and she put
her arms around his neck and looked into Chadwick's eyes,
and they started to kiss, while holding each other very tightly,
and he could feel her hot breath and tongue tingling inside
of his mouth as Tracy kissed him, and chills ran down his
back as Tracy touched his tongue with hers and Chadwick
ran his right hand up the back of Tracy's skirt, caressing her
rounded ass through her silk panties, and Tracy moaned,
and told Chadwick not to stop, as Chadwick felt excited and
could feel her soft hand touching him, through his pants,
and with her other hand rubbing his ripped muscled chest as
she unbuttoned his shirt, Tracy said that she wanted to feel
all him inside of her because she loves him, and Chadwick
put his big fingers in the waistband of Tracy's silk
panties and slowly pulled them down, under
her skirt, and Tracy kicked them to
one side, and laid down on the

deck floor, pulling Chadwick on top of her, and with her legs spread, Chadwick penetrated her tight body as Tracy wrapped her legs around Chadwick pulling him even deeper inside of her wet wanting body, and with every thrust, Chadwick could hear Tracy scream and pant, with pleasure, until they both reached the height and depth of their ecstasy and they both climaxed at the same time, and afterwards, they both composed themselves, and finished dressing themselves and held each other while looking at the night on the ocean.

And Chadwick started walking with Tracy back to her cabin and Tracy said that she could use a drink so once on the Lido Deck they went into the only place that was still open at that hour on the ship, the coffee shop. Chadwick and Tracy went inside and had a cup of hot coco and ate some donuts and talked about the wonderful time that they both were having and hoped that it would never end and afterwards Chadwick walked Tracy back to her cabin and kissed and hugged good night and then Chadwick walked back to his cabin.

CHAPTER
5/DAY FIVE

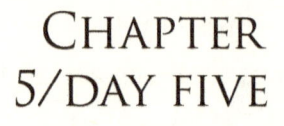

September 5, 1955, Another day at sea on the Atlantic Ocean, Chadwick and his mother spend a quiet day on the lido deck where the sky was overcast, but Chadwick still wore his sunglasses and Chadwick told his mother that he thinks only of Tracy when he is alone and thinks she might be the key to solving his problem and his mother agrees and said that she hopes that things will work out between them.

Chadwick looked up and noticed a couple walking toward them, and it was a man and a lady holding hands, and as they approached, a man who looked to be in his late fifties, spoke, and asked Chadwick, if he and his mother would like to play shuffleboard with he and his wife, Chadwick and his mother agree to play and the man said that his name was Richard McKinney, and that his wife's name was Ellen, and that they were on the cruise to celebrate their thirty fifth wedding anniversary, and went on to say that they had four kids, who were all grown up, and three granddaughters, and one grandson, and Chadwick introduced himself and his mother in courtesy and they started playing shuffleboard, and afterwards, Chadwick and his mother shook hands with the couple and wished them well and then left the area.

Chadwick and his mother started walking back to their room to get dressed for dinner and once inside their cabin.

Chadwick put on his brown suit paired with a white shirt and a brown bow tie with white stripes and his mother put on a yellow long dress with a big bow in the back, and they started walking up to the main dining room, and on the way to dinner about fifteen doors down from their room, Chadwick noticed a beautiful dark haired young lady who looked to be in her 20's coming out of her cabin, and she was wearing a green skirt and had very long hair, and had an amazing figure, and just smiled when Chadwick and his mother walked by her.

Chadwick's heart was pumping and felt the insatiable urge to go on a hunt and like an out of control ulcer raging in the pit of his stomach, he found himself fighting within, to gain control and for a moment his eyes were lit amber, and he noticed his fangs moving in and out, but slowly after regaining control, Chadwick and his mother went to the main dining room to have dinner.

And after entering the main dining room they saw that Tracy and her mother were already there so they joined them. after seating his mother Chadwick sat across from Tracy and told her that she looked amazing, while looking into her eyes, Chadwick and Tracy started to converse about what they might want to do after dinner and Tracy was saying what a gloomy day it was on deck and that she and her mother went to a wine tasting event earlier, but stayed in their room most of the day, and Chadwick told Tracy about the couple they had met, who wanted them to play shuffleboard with them while on the Lido Deck earlier, and that he and his mother played, and had a lot of fun, and Chadwick also agreed with Tracy about the gloomy weather and then Chadwick ordered lobster, potatoes, green beans and a bottle of Champagne for their table and after eating, he and Tracy toasted to the great time that they were having while on the cruise ship and toasted to an even better future together, as they smiled at each other while touching glasses and Tracy again told Chadwick that she really liked him a lot and was glad they had met and Chadwick said he also liked her a lot and that she was very nice and was very pretty and that he was also glad they had met and Tracy exclaimed that there is going to be a Comedian by the name of Franky Jones, doing a show in the green room tonight and that he was from Hollywood Ca and was supposed to be very funny and wanted to know if Chadwick would like to go with her to see the show, and Chadwick said sure as long as his mother did not mind.

After dinner, Chadwick and Tracy said goodbye to their mothers and once again, arm in arm, they left the dining room and while talking and laughing, Chadwick told Tracy that they had plenty of time before the start of the Comedy show and asked Tracy if she wanted to go back to the smokestack deck and Tracy beholding a sexy smile agreed with Chadwick so Tracy arm in arm walked up to the smokestack deck and once there found that they were again all alone and Tracy put her arms around Chadwick's neck, and licked her lips, and her lips were shining, and looked deep into Chadwick's eyes

and told him she loved him
and Chadwick who had a lump
in his throat said that he loved her too,
and Tracy pulled him close to her, and they
started kissing and smelling each other, and wildly
hugging each other, and Tracy said she wanted want him
to make love to her, and went on to say, in her soft seductive
voice, that she wanted to feel him deep inside of her, and
Chadwick put his hand up Tracy's skirt, and started caressing
her tight smooth ass, and then slid his fingers inside her silk
panties and while touching her wetness before he entered his
big fore finger, while hearing her moaning and starting to
pant, Chadwick's heart was racing, as he was excited and could
feel her touching his manhood, with her right hand, and at the
same time telling him she wanted all of him, and he laid her
onto the wooden deck floor and slowly pulled down her white
silk panties, and she could feel the motion of his finger while
it was deep inside her, and she gasped, and said "don't stop,
please don't stop" while moaning and panting, and Chadwick
put his head between her legs, and started licking her smooth
thighs and parted the hair with his long tongue, and started
licking as far as his tongue could reach and nibbling on the
area, Tracy was squirming, and saying don't stop
in a begging tone of voice, and then Tracy
said she wanted to feel his big hard
erection throbbing inside her,

and Chadwick turned Tracy around, and she bent over, and while on her knees Chadwick lifted her skirt showing off her smooth rounded alabaster ass, and he touched his rock hard manhood to her dripping wet skin, and penetrated her tight hot body, as she yelled out with pleasure, and they made love to the sound of the waves slapping against the ship, until they both reached ecstasy to the fullest, and, Tracy was panting like a dog as he exploded inside her warm body, and Chadwick pulled out and was dripping onto Tracy's perfect ass, and she screamed with passion and strangely enough Chadwick noticed that when he is with Tracy that he did not feel the need to hunt and his fangs did not come out and his eyes did not turn amber so he now knew that he was truly in love, and also knew that his problem could be controlled," but he also knew that he had a long way to go before he could get rid of the vampire curse, that had haunted him every day of his adult life.

And after he and Tracy made love they both embraced and held each other for about ten minutes, and then after getting dressed, they walked down to the green room to the comedy show and they sat at a table and had a mixed drink, and while looking into each other's eyes, smiling to each other knowing they had something special.

The comedy show was great, and they both laughed out loud, as others did the same, and after the show was over, they both walked around the floating city together, holding each other, and kissing from time to time, and Tracy told Chadwick that she was having the time of her life, and hoped it would never end, and Chadwick said he too was having the best time ever, and hoped that they would keep seeing each other even after the Cruise had ended.

Chadwick walked Tracy back to her room and kissed her good night and then headed back to he and his mothers room and on the way to his room in the hallway he saw the young lady whom he had seen earlier, "when he and his mother was walking up to dinner," she looked to be in her twenties and was wearing a solid red skirt just above the knees, and a white tight blouse showing off her big upper torso, and her hair was hanging down, Chadwick noticed that she was trying to unlock her cabin door, that was located about fifteen doors down from his room, and as Chadwick got closer to the young lady, she looked up at him with her big blue eyes, and explained that she was having trouble opening her door, and asked if he would help her, and Chadwick said with a big smile, sure, and he opened the young lady's door, and the young lady thanked him, and

as if she was hypnotized she
invited him inside, and Chadwick
said maybe for a little while, and went
into the young ladies room, the room was messed
up with panties and socks and other clothes scattered
on the floor, and she poured them both some type of a drink,
and said her name was Dorothy Wolfe, and that she was on
the cruise with her two friends, who were now out with their
boyfriends, whom they had met while on the cruise, and most
likely wouldn't be back for a couple of hours, and "Chadwick
was shaking, knowing that if he stayed much longer, that the
young lady might be his next victim," and he told the young
lady that he had better go, and to his amazement, the young lady
placed Chadwick's right hand on her large firm left breast, and
put her left hand between his legs, and said come on you know
you want me tiger, and that she could see it in his eyes, and like
an out of control madman, Chadwick ripped off her red skirt,
and tore off her red silk panties, and she removed her bra, and
he threw the young lady onto her her bed, and pounced on her,
like a leopard on a fawn, and she was panting and groaning as
Chadwick turned her over and with her ass in the air, he jammed
his erection deep inside her ass, and she screamed, it hurts,
and it feels good, and don't stop, and in her panting
voice said that he is so big, then he pulled of
her tight ass, and turned her around and
while laying between her legs,

he penetrated her tight young body, as he entered deep inside her, and they made love in all positions imaginable as their sweaty bodies were rolling side to side and they were smelling and tasting each other's sweat and then he exploded deep inside her, like an atomic bomb, and she screamed with passion, and he felt his fangs appearing, and like an alcoholic thrusting for a drink, he yearned for the taste of the young lady's blood, and his eyes lit amber, and he started to penetrate her neck, when they heard a knock at the door, "we're back as they heard two of the other young ladies yell in a slurred speech," so Chadwick got off of the young lady, and put on his pants, and tucked in his shirt, and said he had to go, and the young lady said yes that she understood and thanked him for the great time not knowing she had almost met her demise, she said she would catch up to him later on the Cruise, and Chadwick left the room and went to roam around the big ship, instead of going back to his room, and after going up to the Lido Deck Chadwick again found himself at the bow of the ship leaning over the rails, and looking into the water and her began to reminisce about another hunt.

Chadwick remembered that while he was on the prowl in Chicago, Chadwick ventured out into the big city and came upon what appeared to be a tattoo and massage parlor, and he went inside, and saw a young lady behind the desk, she was very pretty and well-built and she said her name was Tina, and asked how she could be of help, and Chadwick said that he wanted to see if he could get a massage from one of the pretty ladies there and Tina said that it would cost ten dollars for one hour and that she could give him the massage. Chadwick gave the young lady a crisp ten-dollar bill, and she invited him to come into the backroom. Chadwick followed the young lady into the room, that was well lit with off white color walls, and some cabinets on the floor against the wall, and a massage table in the center, and she turned around and locked the door, saying that would keep anyone from just walking in on them, while he was getting his massage, and she had Chadwick to start getting undress, while she went into the other room and said she had to change into her working uniform, and after undressing, Chadwick laid on the table and partly covered himself with a towel, and in about five minutes, Tina came back into the room wearing a very short white dress, showing off her sexy tan legs, and she began to massage Chadwick's back, and legs, but he couldn't help but to look up her skirt time to time as she was bending over and while showing her white silky panties, and she put some hot type of oil on her hands and it felt really great, as

she started rubbing him all
over and even under the towel
that was partly covering his nude body,
and said in a sexy tone of voice "does that feel
good?" and Chadwick said "yes and that she was very
good" and then she told Chadwick to turn around, and
Chadwick turned around with the towel just covering his
private parts, and Tina was smiling and put some more hot oil
in her right hand, and rubbed her hands together, and started
massaging his muscular hairy chest, and then she moved her
hand under the towel and started massaging him, and at
this time after looking at her long legs and beautiful figure,
Chadwick was getting excited, and it showed, and she said in
a seductive voice "oh my what do we have here", as she is still
massaging underneath of the towel, and she said "do you want
me to get on top of you" and Chadwick said yes please and
the young lady put her hands up her dress and bent over and
pulled down her silky white panties, while showing Chadwick
her bare rounded ass, and the patch of hair between her
legs, and then she straddled Chadwick while he was still
on the massage table, and she slowly guided his rock hard
erection up inside her wet dripping body, and rode him like
a stud at a rodeo, while panting and moaning, and
saying that she loved him inside her, until he
exploded inside her, hot body, while
she was panting, and moaning,

but then Chadwick felt his fangs coming out of his gums, and his eyes lit amber, and he grabbed the young ladies hair and as she screamed and hit him with her fist and grabbed his arm and was biting him trying to get away as his fangs penetrated her neck, and blood went everywhere, and the white sheet on the table and her white dress was covered with blood, as Chadwick fed on the young lady and then left in a flash.

And Chadwick stopped remembering and then walked back to he and his mother's room and his mother who was still awake asked Chadwick if he and Tracy had a good time at the show, and Chadwick said that they had wonderful time and that he now knew for sure that he loved Tracy more than life itself and that she loves him as much and that they have so much in common and understood each other, and almost as if they were made for each other and Chadwick went on to say he could hardly wait to meet with the Madam, and hopefully get rid of the curse of the vampire that has been torching him inside so that he can live a normal life, and maybe he and Tracy could get married and he would not feel like a murdering freak and then Chadwick and his mother turned in for the night.

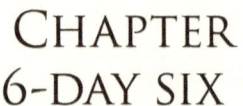

CHAPTER
6-DAY SIX

September 6th 1955, the sixth day of the cruise Chadwick was very excited in knowing that he would be meeting with Madam Medina in the evening, so he was up and out of bed before noon, and his mother told him that he looked chipper today, and Chadwick replied that he was looking forward to meeting with the Madam tonight and then he and his mother went out for lunch, and on the way to lunch they stopped by the Blue Room to view an art show, the blue room was well lit, painted royal blue and had all types of paintings on aisles surrounding the whole room, they enjoyed the champagne and admired some of the art in the room, and his mother bought a painting of a Swiss lady standing in front of a windmill, " I'll put this in the family room she said", and Chadwick agreed that it would look good there and then he and his mother left the blue room.

After leaving the blue room, Chadwick and his mother walked up to the main dining room to have lunch and after seating his mother, Chadwick had the special soup of the day, a sandwich and tea and his mother had the same. After eating and talking for a while, Chadwick and his Mother went back to their cabin and Chadwick told his Mother that he was so glad that they had gone on this cruise and that so far, he was having a great time.

After going to their room to sleep and rest for a few hours, Chadwick and his mother started getting ready for dinner. His mother put on a green skirt, white blouse and tied a scarf around her neck while Chadwick put on his tan suit with a white shirt and a brown tie with acorns on it and his brown leather buckle shoes and then they left to go up to the main dining room for dinner, and like before when they entered the dining room they found that Tracy and her mother was already there so Chadwick seated his mother and

sat down across from Tracy
and told Tracy she looked very
lovely tonight and Tracy smiled, made
intense eye contact and thanked Chadwick and
Tracy asked Chadwick if he wanted to go back to
the smokestack deck tonight, and Chadwick said yes but
it would have to be later, maybe at around 11 P.M., because
he and his mother were going to spend some time together,
knowing that he and his mother had an appointment with
the Madam tonight and Tracy said that is was fine and that
she would see him at the smokestack deck at 11pm then they
conversed, ate and then went their separate ways.

Chadwick and his mother walked up to the upper deck
to Madam Medina's room, number U-66 and Chadwick
knocked on the door and heard a growing voice say, "come
in its open" and Chadwick and his mother entered the
room. The Madam had a nice cabin with a table and chairs
and a couch off to one side, and said "sit down and make
yourselves at home", as she poured them some hot green tea
and Chadwick noticed that the Madam had a little black
box in the middle of the table, in her cabin that was just like
the one he had seen earlier in her shows, and after they
drank the tea, Chadwick's mother agreed to pay
the Madam the amount of $1,000 for now

and $5,000 at the end of the Cruise if Chadwick's problem was solved.

The Madam asked Chadwick's mother if she would leave the room because she needed to be alone with Chadwick to be able to help so his mother left and stated that she would see him later in there room and after his mother left, the Madam asked Chadwick if he had the urge to hunt or if he went on a hunt since he had been aboard the ship and the Madam explained that he must be completely honest with her if she was to help him and so Chadwick told her that he had somewhat of a hunt last night and explained about the young lady in the cabin who was drunk and was staying just 15 rooms down from their room and that her friends interrupted them before he could finish, and the Madam agreed that it was a good thing that the other ladies showed up and Chadwick also told the Madam about the new love in his life. He shared all the experiences he has had with Tracy so far and the Madam then told Chadwick to look deep into her eyes and not to be afraid, and after making eye contact, Chadwick went into some type of trance, but remained alert as to his surroundings, but he could not move and found that her eyes were like windows, that he was looking through instead of looking into a pair of dark eyes and the

Madam started chanting and saying some type of incantation and he could see a part of his past while looking into the eyes of the Madam, and then the Madam started to wave her hands again over the little black box. It was very dark in the room, and he could see some type of red fog coming out of the box as the Madam chanted louder and louder, and then she stopped chanting and said, "Chadwick from here on out you will think only happy thoughts, and will not have the urge to hunt and if you feel the urge coming, you will only think of the ones you love and the ones that love you."

After about an hour into the session the Madam snapped her fingers, and Chadwick came out of the trance and was now able to move. Chadwick was feeling really good, but the Madam said that he had to be careful this is a critical time, and that he needed to do his part, and she had given him some mental exercises to do every night and during the day when he was alone, the Madam told Chadwick that she would meet with him again on September 10th at the same time and Chadwick shook hands with the Madam. He left and went back to the cabin.

Once inside the cabin Chadwick explained to his mother that he now feels better than ever, especially after the meeting with the Madam, and told her about their next meeting, on September 10th at 8 P.M.

After he spent some time with his mother in their cabin, conversing to her what he and the Madam talked about, Chadwick freshened up and left and said that he was going to meet with Tracy and after running up the steps, and onto the smokestack deck, thinking of Tracy in each step that he took, he was out of breath as he gazed at the ocean waves thinking that he could not wait to see Tracy again and after a while Chadwick heard someone coming and it was Tracy coming up the steps to the smokestack deck, which was now presumably coined their special meeting place and Tracy asks Chadwick, how his evening went and Chadwick said that it was great and that he and his mother had spent some time together and Tracy put her arms around Chadwick's neck and he could smell her natural scent and perfume, as Tracy said how much she had missed being with him and how much she loves everything about him. Chadwick told Tracy that she smelled really good next to him. Tracy was wearing a ruffled just above the knee black skirt, and a red flowered form fitting blouse and Chadwick pulled her closer and as they gazed into each other's eyes, they kissed, and caressed each other and touched each other's most special places, Chadwick opened her button up red flowered blouse and pulled out one of her large breasts from her white lace bra, and started licking her nipple, and as she gasped and she said that she wanted him so he put his right hand up the front of her skirt and could feel the wetness between her legs through her panties and was about to make passionate love until they heard someone coming up the steps and so they reluctantly had to stop their fiery passion and after they quickly composing themselves, they heard a voice say "nice evening isn't it, "and they both said yes it is, and left arm in arm while laughing about almost getting caught and they then walked all around the ship and were kissing at every chance, and then Chadwick walked Tracy to her room, and they embraced and neither wanted to let the other go, but Tracy finally decided to go back into her cabin and Chadwick walked back up to the lido deck and to the bow of the big ship.

Once at the bow of the big ship, Chadwick again leaned over the railing and was looking deep into the ocean as he started to remember his past. It happened in fall and the leaves were turning color and Chadwick was around twenty two years old and he had went out for a stroll in the neighborhood, and came up to a cottage, that had a picket fence, and noticed a young lady who was raking some of the fallen leaves from a maple tree that was next to her cottage, and just as he was passing, the young lady looked up at Chadwick, and jokingly asked if he wanted to help her with the leaves and said that her name was Dorothy Gordon, she looked to be in her late twenties and was wearing knee knockers, a plaid shirt, sneakers and had her long brown hair tied back in a ponytail and Chadwick being the gentleman that he is said sure he would love help her with the leaves and entered the yard and after opening the gate in the picket fence, Chadwick shook hands with her and told her that his name was Chadwick Burnouf and that he was single, lives with his mother, and that he was just out for a stroll and Dorothy also told Chadwick that she was a widower, and that her husband who was in the Army had been killed in an accident while on maneuvers one night while he was sleeping, an army tank had ran over him and crushed him to death, and that it had happened about three years ago, and she went on to say, that ever since that tragic day, she has been living by herself because she does not have any relatives or friends in the area, and that she was originally from New Mexico, and that it was her husband's career had brought her to Chicago.

And after raking for about
an hour, sweating and talking,
Chadwick finally helped Dorothy fill
the last bag, with leaves. Afterwards Dorothy
invited Chadwick to come inside for refreshments and
Chadwick went into the lady's residence, it was very clean,
with a beautiful blue carpet and a brown couch and chair, and
two end tables with lamps in the living room, and he saw that
the lady must have really loved her husband because there was
pictures of them everywhere.

After drinking a glass of cola, Dorothy said that she was
going to freshen up, and went into the bathroom. Chadwick
heard the sound of a shower running and Dorothy came out
only wearing a towel and a smile and asked Chadwick if he
too wanted to freshen up since he was sweaty after helping
her with the leaves and Dorothy said while smiling that the
shower had room for two and so Chadwick started getting
undressed. He unbuttoned his shirt, showing off his rippling
back and chest muscles and laid his shirt at the back of the
couch and unzipped his pants and took off his white boxer
shorts, showing off his manly physique and found himself
in the shower with Dorothy, and they started to wash
each other, Chadwick washed Dorothy's breast
and reached around and lathered up her
ass, as he washed and copped a feel

in every stroke and Dorothy
lathered up Chadwick's muscular
hairy chest and got down on her knees
and took his large erection in both hands and
put the tip into her drooling mouth and was now
tasting something that she had not had for three years and
was enjoying every moment of it, while she was going back
and forth Chadwick was holding her head and pulling her
closer after Chadwick exploded in her mouth and filled her
throat and she stood up and Chadwick noticed her big plump
breast and he started nibbling and licking around Dorothy's
nipple, "and he could tell, that Dorothy had not been with a
man for a while", she was like a caged animal, grabbing him
and panting and moaning, while telling him in a panting
voice, that she wanted him inside her, and then she bent over,
reaching around and grabbing Chadwick, and pulled him
closer, as his large erection penetrated her hot body like an ax
splitting an oak, she screamed out loud as she was experiencing
pleasure and pain she had never felt in so long, and said that
it hurts, but please do not stop and she panted to the rhythm
of his back and forth motion, as he went deeper inside of
her warm wet body, and while the water was beading and
running down her rounded white ass cheeks, and
after making love for about an hour and like
dynamite in a mining hole, Chadwick
exploded deep inside of her hot

wanting body and Dorothy screamed and moaned with pleasure and then they embraced with the shower still running and unbeknownst to Dorothy, Chadwick's eyes lit amber and he started to drool like a sick wolf and his heart was beating fast, his fangs appeared, and with his mouth wide open and Dorothy holding him close, he scraped his fangs against her soft wet neck, and bit down hard, and Dorothy started to scream very loudly, the blood squirted out like a fountain while Chadwick was feasting like a fox in a hen house and the shower looked like a bloody mess. Chadwick remembered leaving the lady lying on the shower floor and the water still running then he left the lady's house in a flash and went home and later remembering how bad he felt knowing that he may have killed another person or turned them into a vampire.

And then Chadwick, stopped reminiscing, and found himself leaning over the rail of the ship in tears and knowing that he had to get rid of the vampire curse that haunted him, and hoped that the Madam can really help him, because he hated that side of himself and wanted only to live a happy and normal life and then he then left the area and walked back to his cabin...

CHAPTER
7-DAY SEVEN

September 7th 1955, another beautiful day at sea and waiting to port in Southampton, England, it was now around 4:00 P.M. Chadwick and his mother started getting ready for dinner after sleeping most of the day and Chadwick had been doing some of his mental activities that the Madam had prescribed for him then after bathing, Chadwick put on his pin striped blue suit, a yellow shirt and a brown tie with his lace up brown shoes while his mother wore a yellow dress with a pink bow in the center and also wore a beaded necklace and then he and his mother started walking up to the main dining room and since the ship was now in port, they were excited about getting to see the majesties of England and could not wait until tomorrow to go touring and sightseeing and when they entered the main dining room, They saw Tracy's mother was seated, but Tracy herself was not there and her mother said that the reason why was because Tracy was not feeling very well and had a light fever as well as stomach cramps and was still in their cabin and that she wanted Chadwick to visit her after dinner, if he would and Chadwick happily agreed and said he would love to and they all ate dinner and conversed about being in England and being at the same port where the Titanic was ported before departing for New York in 1912 and went on to say as to how great the show was last night and that Madam Medina was going to be on tonight in the green room and so Naomi and Tracy's mother decided to go together since Chadwick was going to be visiting Tracy in her cabin.

At 7:45 P.M. They all left the main dining area and Chadwick while walking to Tracy's Cabin stopped by one of the little shops along the way, and picked up some silk roses, a box of candy as well as a get well soon card, and then proceeded toward Tracy's cabin.

Chadwick knocked on Tracy's door and she invited him to come in and Chadwick entered the room and told Tracy that he had missed seeing her at dinner tonight and that her mother had told him she was feeling ill and so Chadwick gave Tracy the silk flowers, candy and the get well soon card. She opened the card and read it and thanked him especially for the flowers and candy and said that she loved him very much and Chadwick asked Tracy how she was feeling tonight and Tracy said a lot better since he was there and should be better by tomorrow and that the on board doctor gave her some pills and said for her to stay in her room tonight. Chadwick and Tracy talked about her wanting to be a nurse and Chadwick spoke about him becoming a play writer someday and also wanted to become a Philanthropist, since he also wanted to be able to help people and said how much he loved to travel. Chadwick leaned in and kissed Tracy on the forehead, and told her he loved her a lot and couldn't wait until tomorrow so he and Tracy could roam the ship again and possibly they could see England together and how romantic it was, porting in the same location as the Titanic, when it had left on its final voyage in 1912 and how it compared to the ship they were now on, they also talked about as to what a tragedy it was and they conversed about all of the

history behind it and Tracy
agreed as Chadwick held Tracy
in his strong arms, and they closed their
eyes, and were now in their own little world
and they kissed again and Tracy told Chadwick that
she was thinking of changing schools and possibly going to
nursing School in Chicago, so they would be seeing a lot of
each other after the cruise ends and Chadwick was so glad
and excited to hear that because Chadwick wanted to tell
Tracy everything about the struggle, about the curse that he
has inside him to become a vampire, but at the same time he
knows that he would risk losing her and that no one could
understand his problem, but maybe when he is cured and the
curse is removed then he could then tell her the truth.

After about two hours in Tracy's cabin, Chadwick kissed
Tracy and hugged her and told her to get well soon and then
he left so she could get some rest and then Chadwick went
up to the Lido deck to get a cup of coffee and to smoke a
cigar he had bought from the Island earlier in the week and
Chadwick sat down at a table on the port side of the ship
that was overlooking Southampton and while sitting there
enjoying a steaming cup of coffee, and watching the
lights off of the shore of South Hampton glowing
in the water on this moonlit night, he
pulled out a Churchill size cigar

and cut off the end and lit
it with a match and he noticed
a man walking over toward his table
that was next to the railing on the Lido Deck
and the man was well dressed, and looked to be in his
late thirties, and the man approached him, and said that his
name was Sam Pyle and Chadwick while shaking the man's
hand introduced himself and Sam asks Chadwick if he was
having a nice cruise and Chadwick said yes, and went on to
say that he was having a wonderful time so far, and couldn't
wait to see England tomorrow, and the man told Chadwick,
that he and his wife was also having a great time, and that this
was his fourth cruise, and that his wife Diana, had went to
the Madam Medina show tonight, and that she was to meet
him later on the Lido Deck when the show was over, and Sam
went on to tell Chadwick, that he never understood that type
of witchcraft and magic voodoo.

After sitting down across from Chadwick, Sam also pulled
out a cigar, bit off the end and lit it with a fancy silver lighter
and blew out the flame and asked Chadwick if he minded
if he joined him and Chadwick said he did not mind at all
and would appreciate the company since he was alone.
Sam was drinking some type of mixed drink
that was in a stem glass, and went on to
say that he was a criminal Lawyer

and was from New York City and that he and his wife was on their second honeymoon and they also wanted to get away from the rat race in New York City and fighting the traffic in the crowded concrete jungle and said that they were really enjoying the slow pace while on the cruise ship, and Sam asked Chadwick if he was married and Chadwick replied that he was not but he had met a beautiful young girl while on the ship and thinks that he is in love with her and that she was a bit under the weather tonight and should be back to normal by tomorrow and after about a half an hour Chadwick shook hands with the man and wished him well, and Sam did the same, afterwards Chadwick left the area.

Chadwick again found himself at the bow of the ship while watching the lights from the shore dancing on the water, as he was thinking about how much he cared about Tracy and thought about how nice it could be if they were to be married and could live a normal life and have a house with a picket fence, and kids, but he wonders if all that he wants is only something he can dream about.

Chadwick while holding on to the rails with both hands started to remember a time he and his mother went to visit New York City wherein they traveled by Greyhound bus and Chadwick remembered staying in a high rise hotel overlooking the New York Skyline, and while in New York, he and his mother, while sightseeing went on a subway ride and went shopping at Macy's Store, and talked about Macy's parade and the Christmas shows that surrounded it and later they took a Ferry across the bay and went to see and tour the Statue of Liberty. It was gigantic and they went inside and went up several flights of steps and walked out onto the torch and they could see the vastness of the world around them. Afterwards, Chadwick and his mother went back to their hotel room and later that night at around midnight, Chadwick was on the prowl and left the hotel room and was walking around and found himself at a nightclub, it was wild, everyone was drinking, smoking, dancing and the ladies pulling up their skirts, showing off their silk panties and Chadwick had a drink in one hand and a lit cigarette in the other hand and noticed a lady that looked to be in her late twenties or early thirties sash shade over to where he was leaning against the bar and she was very pretty and had long black hair and her lips glistened red and she had on a black low cut dress showing off some of her plump breast and she spoke to Chadwick and said in a sexy voice, that her name was Roxanne, but she liked to be called Roxie and

Chadwick introduced himself as well and she asked him if he wanted to dance, and Chadwick said sure and they went onto the dance floor and a slow song was playing while Chadwick and Roxie was dancing very closely and she whispered into Chadwick's ear and asked if he wanted to engage in something very sensual and Chadwick said, yes but definitely not on the dance floor and Roxie laughed and said "no silly, we can go in back room", but said that it would cost him $10 to get into her panties, and Chadwick gave the lady a new $10 bill, and she grabbed his hand and lead him into the backroom, it was dark and badly lit and there was a couch against the wall and once inside she locked the door behind her and started taking off her fitting black dress, relieving her light blue silky panties and bra, while showing off her perfect nude body, and she grabbed Chadwick and started unzipping him and took out his large erect manhood and her eyes were drawn instantly to it because she saw how big he was and she put it deep into her mouth while wrapping her wet tongue around it and holding it in her hand then she pulled back and arose to her feet, and laid back onto the couch while spreading her legs showing Chadwick all of her wetness between the patch of hair between her legs and she used her thumb and forefinger to spread apart the skin and at the same time pulling Chadwick on top of her and scratched his back as he penetrated her petite little body and with her legs wrapped around him and pulling him deeper inside her, she was panting as Chadwick climaxed and then she turned around and got on her knees with her back side showing off her smooth rounded ass, and said in her sexy voice that she wanted to feel him screwing her in her tight ass as she pulled back her cheeks with both hands and from behind Chadwick thrust inside her wanting hot body and she screamed with pain and pleasure, as Chadwick felt his fangs appearing and was drooling at the mouth, and his eyes lit amber and he grabbed her long hair and pulled her neck back, and bit into the lady's neck so hard that a chunk of skin and bloody muscle came out into his mouth and he exploded inside her hot body as blood was squirting all over and as she screamed very loudly, Chadwick feasted on the lady until he was completely satisfied and then he left in a hurried manner and went back to he and his mother's hotel room. Chadwick remembered another time when he was around twenty three years old and his mother took a four day trip, and flew to San Francisco, California, she said that she had always wanted to see the Golden Gate Bridge and the street cars so they stayed in a nice ten story hotel that overlooked a part of the big city and he remembered

he and his mother riding on
the street car and hearing the
bells when it came to a stop, and they
took a tour of the Golden Gate Bridge.

And on the third night Chadwick remembered
sneaking out of their hotel room and went on the prowl and
he was going floor to floor of the hotel looking for a victim,
while thirsting for blood and when he reached the second
floor, Chadwick got off of the elevator and started walking
around and saw a housekeeping lady, she was wearing a white
uniform type dress and she had short blond hair and was
pushing a housekeeping cart, she stopped just outside of room
211 and started to enter the room and then Chadwick walked
by, brushing the cart and the lady said that she was sorry that
the cart was in the way and Chadwick smiled as he looked
deep into the lady's eyes and said that it was alright and that it
was his fault and the young lady looked at Chadwick as if she
was in some type of a trance and said her name was Lorie and
Chadwick introduced himself and shook her hand and said
that it was very nice meeting her and as if she was hypnotized,
she squeezed and grabbed Chadwick's hand and pulled him
into the room that she was getting ready to clean and
pulled the cart into the room and locked the
door behind her and started hugging and
kissing Chadwick as she pulled him

onto the unmade bed, and said that she had not been with a man for about two years, "and she was hot as a firecracker" because she wanted him to screw the legs off of her and so Chadwick put his big hand up under her white uniform dress and started touching her soft wet skin through her panties as he could feel and smell her warmth then he heard her soft voice saying and, almost begging him not to stop and Chadwick pulled off her white stockings and panties with her legs high in the air and pounced on her like a mountain lion on a fawn and he started licking her toes and working his way up into her thighs licking her and placing his long tongue inside her hot body as she panted and moaned with pleasure and he got on top of her and forced his giant erection deeply inside her body and she screamed with pain and said that it was painful and told him to stop because it was hurting her, but he thrust deeper into her wetness, and like a volcano the erupted and she was now crying in pain on that unmade bed and she groaned and after filling her body, Chadwick pulled out and Chadwick again could feel his fangs moving out of his gums, and his eyes lighting up in the shade of amber and with his mouth opened wide and while Chadwick was holding the lady's arms down to her sides as his fangs penetrated the lady's neck and blood squirted all over her white uniform and she screamed loudly, as he sucked her blood, and afterwards he left the room in a hurry and went back to his hotel room on the ninth floor.

Chadwick stopped remembering and again he hated what he had done, and hoped that the Madam could cure him, so he could live a normal life and then he walked back to his cabin and did the mental exercises the Madam had shown him and later went to sleep after gaining control of the rage that was growing inside him.

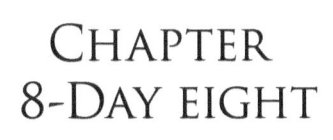

CHAPTER
8-DAY EIGHT

S eptember 8th on this day the M.S.S Goliath was now ported in South Hampton, England. Chadwick and his mother were very excited, and got out of bed early. Chadwick and his mother walked up to the Lido Deck to have breakfast and then they were to meet with Tracy and her mother and afterwards they planned to start touring England and since they would be there for two days, they had a lot of planning to do so after arriving at the Lido Deck and meeting with Tracy and her mother, they ordered breakfast and all sat down at a table that was near the railing where they could

admire the beautiful sunrise
while enjoying their meal.

Tracy was beautiful in her pink shorts
and short sleeved blouse and she had her hair tied
back in a ponytail with a pink ribbon, and after talking
and eating, Chadwick and Tracy and their mother's left the
ship and afterwards Chadwick and Tracy split up from their
mothers and took a cab to tour some of what England had to
offer and while in the cab they conversed about how great it
was being ported in the same port that the Titanic had left
for New York, City back in 1912 and had the taxi driver to
take them to visit the Tower of London and afterwards they
saw Buckingham Palace and went to see the changing of the
guard and they went on a tour to see and look into the history
of Big Ben and then Chadwick and Tracy went walking on
the sidewalk and headed to a street café with outside tables
along the sidewalk, and they lunch there and had a drink.

England was very nice and the people on the streets seemed
proper, speaking as they walked by. The city was very busy
with vehicle traffic and people. Chadwick asked Tracy if she
wanted to go back to the Smoke Stack Deck tonight after
dinner and Tracy replied that she wanted to, but she
could not because she and her mother had to
spend some time together, but maybe
at around 11:30 P.M. When her

mother goes to their room they could get together and Chadwick agreed, "and Tracy also had a secret, and had not been completely honest with Chadwick, as to why she and her mother was on the Cruise, Tracy's father was killed when she was a baby, and she never knew him, but she later learned from her mother that he was not killed in an auto accident, but was killed while on a hunt, see Tracy's father was a Werewolf" and her mother was not and Tracy was only half Werewolf, and had the urge to go on a hunt herself from time to time and had been hunting in Austin, Texas for about three years and wanted to live a normal life and was on the ship to see if Madam Medina could cure her problem and break the curse of the Werewolf and she was to meet with the Madam tonight at around 8:00 P.M. and that's why she couldn't meet with Chadwick after dinner," but she could not tell him her problem because he would never understand and how could he, how could any normal person understand, but she knew she loved Chadwick and she would not do anything to jeopardize that and maybe after she was cured from the beast that kept wanting to take over her body, she could then tell Chadwick."

After a day of touring England full of walking and kissing and holding each other, Chadwick and Tracy, both wanted each other more than ever, Chadwick and Tracy went back to the ship, and started getting ready for dinner and Chadwick told his mother how much he loved Tracy and what a great time they had touring England together. His mother said Tracy's mother was nice as well and they had a great time as well and after getting dressed for dinner Chadwick and his mother went up to the main dining room and after arriving, they found that Tracy and her mother were already seated and Chadwick seated his mother and sat across from Tracy, and again, while looking deeply into each other's eyes conversed about what a great time they had touring England and Tracy said lets toast holding up her wine glass and said "cheers to a wonderful time with great people on this great cruise," and they all touched glasses and sipped their wine and after dinner Tracy and her mother left early while Chadwick and his mother had dessert and coffee, and then talked some more and then left the area.

They went to a Broadway show that was in the Auditorium and after they arrived, they found two seats in front and sat down next to the stage. The singing and dancing was great and the young ladies were beautiful, kicking high, while wearing short skirts and showing off their long smooth legs, and afterwards Chadwick's mother went back to her room

and Chadwick after walking
around the big ship for a while
walked up to the Smoke stack deck, to
wait for Tracy and after waiting for about half
an hour, "which seemed to be forever" Tracy showed
up wearing a knee length gray skirt, with a red blouse and
heels, and after walking over to Chadwick, who was standing
by one of the smoke stacks, they embraced and Tracy pulled
Chadwick close to her, Chadwick could feel her large breast
through her blouse touching his chest, and she started kissing
him, as their tongues touched with a tingling sensation, and
Chadwick was unbuttoning Tracy's blouse while kissing
and licking his way to her juicy plump breast and when he
reached her nipple area, she started groaning and moaning
and Chadwick put his hand up Tracy's skirt and pulled down
her silk panties and got down on his knees and with his head
up her skirt, both of his hands on her round ass, Chadwick
started licking the wetness between Tracy's legs, smelling her
sweet natural body, he slipped his long tongue inside her,
and she gasped, groaned and moaned in passion as he laid
on his back, he could feel the wooden deck now behind him,
while pulling Tracy on top of him and with her legs spread,
Chadwick penetrated her soft hot wet body, and
she screamed in pleasure, and was panting
and would grunt and moan every
time Chadwick would lunge

upward, as they went at it for about 45 minutes, until they both climaxed at the same time, and after getting dressed, they held each other very tightly, telling each other how much they love each other and then Chadwick walked Tracy back to her room.

And then Chadwick walked around the big ship for a while, and then he walked up to the Lido Deck, and found himself again at the bow of the big ship, and while looking over the rail and into the dark water, Chadwick was thinking about himself and Tracy and how much he loves her and how pretty and nice she was and how much they have in common, and hoped that he could be honest enough with her to tell her everything and about him being half vampire, but knowing that if he did, he would risk losing the love of his life, and he hoped that the Madam would be able to remove the curse that was tearing at his soul and hoped that he and Tracy could get married someday as he cried into the ocean and then Chadwick walked back to his room and went past the casino, and stopped by and put some coins into the slot machine, but never won anything, and then he walked back to his room for the night.

After about an hour Tracy left her room on this full moon lit night to go for a walk because she could not sleep and found herself looking off of the ship and she noticed a young man who was on the dock and was wearing a plain white shirt, jeans and smoking while leaning over the rail on the dock and looking into the water, and Tracy's eyes lit greenish yellow and her face began to stretch into a form of a beast, she was drooling like a mad dog, as she began to transform into a werewolf and like a gazelle she leaped off of the upper deck of the big ship and onto the dock and in one motion her one inch canine type teeth entered the young man's neck, while biting off his head as it fell into the water and she feasted on the young man's flesh like a caveman whom hadn't eaten in a month and she was lapping up the blood as she striped away the skin until she was completely satisfied and then in a flash she left the area and went back to her and her mother's cabin to clean up and later hated herself for what she had done.

Another time Tracy remembered when she and a friend went to a Fraternity party that was at a University that her girlfriend had attended, and on this night they all were drinking and smoking, and just about everyone there was either drunk or well on their way to getting drunk, and it was a full moon lit night, and at around midnight, Tracy and a young man that she had met at the party, whose name was Stephen Foster went into the back room area, it appeared to be some type of storage room, it was drab and there was boxes all around, and once inside he turned and locked the metal door and they were all alone and after hugging and kissing, Stephen slapped Tracy across the face, making a red mark on her right cheek, and grabbed her shoulders with both hands and threw her down onto the floor and put his hand up her skirt and into her silk panties while forcing his finger inside her and said in a slurred tone voice, he said that he knows that she wanted him and Tracy repeatedly said no, but Stephen proceeded with his mission, of trying to rape her and like a mad bull, Tracy moved her legs and lunged in an upward thrust and threw him into the air so hard that he hit the nine foot ceiling and fell hard onto the floor crushing the young man's skull while at the same time Tracy was transforming into a Werewolf and with her elongated toothy mouth opened wide, she bit the young man's head completely off and began to feast, and then she went on a rage out into the party area, clearing out most of the people and slaughtering, anyone that got in her way or those that she had made contact with and leaving behind several victims, some dead and some just bleeding and some without limbs, it was a drunk and bloody mess with people screaming, and running to get away from this mad monster.

Tracy stopped reminiscing, as she had felt bad for what she had done, and the people that she had hurt, even the young man who tried to take advantage of her. So she turned in for the night and went to sleep crying.

CHAPTER
9 – DAY NINE

September 9th, the ninth day of the Cruise and while still in Southampton, England Chadwick and his mother were eating lunch and heard about the person who was killed the night before, they overheard another passenger say that a man was smoking on the dock and was murdered and that some people heard a howling sound just before the body was found. Chadwick said that he and his mother should be careful when touring since there was a murderer in the area, Chadwick's mother asked Chadwick if Tracy was going to be joining them for lunch and Chadwick said "I don't think she will" and that he had met with Tracy after his mother went back to her room last night, Chadwick also told his mother that he is in love with Tracy and could not wait until he was completely cured so he could live a normal life and he also told his mother that Tracy wanted to transfer to Chicago to finish out her schooling and that they would be able to spend time together after the cruise and his mother was so glad for her son.

Chadwick and his mother left the ship at around 1:30 P.M. so they could spend some time together touring England, they also went to the Tower of London and Buckingham Palace, saw the changing of the guard again, and then they took a cab and went out into the countryside, and saw some of the old structures, some of the cassels and buildings were hundreds of years old, it was a beautiful day and while in the country they decided to go to an old winery and tasted various wines and bought one bottle of white wine and one bottle of red wine to take back to the ship and then they went back to South Hampton and did some shopping in some of the smaller stores and then headed back to the ship. Chadwick and his mother relaxed the rest of the day and at around 4:30 P.M. He and his mother started getting dressed for dinner. The theme was a special black-tie night for everyone on the cruise so Chadwick put on his black tuxedo with a black bow tie and and vest, and black shoes and his mother put on a black gown and tied her hair back with a sparkling diamond hair comb and at around 5:30 P.M. They headed up to the main dining room for dinner and after seating his mother Chadwick sat down and then Tracy and her mother came in, Tracy looked delightful in a pink sparkling gown which hugged her beautiful body and her hair down and Chadwick seated Tracy and her mother and one of the servers came over and said his name was Zeya and he would be working their table tonight, he had a European accent and was dressed in a white tuxedo and opened up a bottle of chilled red wine and started pouring it into the ladies wine glasses first after Chadwick had tested and approved of the vintage. Chadwick's mother said "did you hear about the murder last night near the Cruise ship on the dock", and Tracy's mother said they did hear about it and went on to change the subject, knowing that it was Tracy who had committed the murder, but also knowing her daughter was not a murderer, and was only trying to get help for her problem, Tracy also changed the subject and asked Chadwick if they could walk around the ship after dinner before going to the ship's ball in the main auditorium which starts at 10:00 P.M. Chadwick agreed and they conversed some more about the tour they had taken, Chadwick had a thick lean steak, baked beans and a wedding soup. After dinner Chadwick and Tracy left the main dining room and walked around and Chadwick again brought up the murder that had taken place on the dock and again Tracy changed the subject and then they proceeded to the smoke stack deck where they knew they could spend some time alone.

Once at the smokestack deck, Tracy put her arms around Chadwick and pulled him close to her and Chadwick's heart was racing as he pushed his lips against Tracy's luscious wet lips and their tongues touched and like a bear lapping honey they kissed and hugged one another and Tracy said that she wanted to feel Chadwick inside her and that she loved him very much and Chadwick slid his hand down the back of Tracy's pink gown and grabbed her ass while still kissing her and she said she did not want to get her gown dirty, so she turned around and with both hands raised her gown and held it up past her waist line and bends over showing a part of her ass that looked to be busting out of her tight fitting pink panties and Chadwick put his fingers into the waistband and pulled her panties down to her knees, showing off her wetness peeping through her patch of hair and then Chadwick unzipped his pants and pulled out his large erection and moved into her, parting her skin as he penetrated her warm wet wanting body and as he was ramming deep, he could hear her panting to the rhythm of his back and forth motion and she groaned every time he would slap her ass and telling him it feels good and not to stop in her panting tone of voice as their sweating bodies came together as one and like animals they made passionate love for about 45 minutes and then composed themselves and headed to the ballroom, arm in arm and kissing whenever possible and Chadwick said that he loved Tracy more than life itself and hoped they would always be together and Tracy concurred and after entering the ballroom, Tracy and Chadwick found a seat at a table where their mothers were waiting and Chadwick's mother said, "where have you kids been?" and Chadwick said that they were just walking around the ship and star watching and then Chadwick asked Tracy's mother if she wanted to dance, and she said "sure I would love to" and they went onto the dance floor and she was a great dancer and Tracy's mother explained that she was glad they decided to go on this Cruise and was glad Tracy had met a nice man and Chadwick explained that he felt the same and was having the time of his life, and hoped he and Tracy could see more of each other after the cruise.

After the dance Chadwick walked Tracy's mother back to their table and asked his mother if she would like to dance, she said "no, but I'm sure Tracy would" and Tracy said "let's go" and Chadwick took her soft hand and they went onto the dance floor and danced very closely as he could smell her wonderful scent, and at one point he nibbled on her neck and Tracy whispered into Chadwick's ear that she loved him, afterwards they all left the ballroom and Chadwick and Tracy went on their own to explore some more of the ship and to star gaze, Tracy told Chadwick that one day she had something important to tell him, something only she and her mother knew and when the time was right she would tell him and Chadwick also told Tracy that he too had something to explain to her when the time was right and they went on to say how much they both had in common and that they must be meant for each other. It seemed like their meeting on the cruise was a case of serendipity, it was almost midnight when Chadwick walked Tracy back to her room, again standing outside the room after making eye contact they started kissing and hugging each other and not wanting to let go, but Chadwick reluctantly left and went up to the lido deck.

And he walked to the bow of the ship and leaned over the railing looking at the lighted city of South Hampton and again Chadwick began to reminisce about another time he had went on a hunt, it was when he and his mother were visiting friends in Milwaukee back in December, it was very cold on this full moon lit night and Chadwick had went for a walk down the street and found himself outside a residence where he had seen a young lady and her boyfriend building a snowman days before. When he got to the residence, he saw the young man leaving, thinking he was going to work.

She was very pretty with long red hair and after watching the young lady's house and watching her man leave, Chadwick went up to the door and knocked and said his car had broken down and asked if he could use her phone and the young lady who was wearing a knee length robe invited him to come in and her eyes looked as if she was in a trance and once inside the young lady's two story brown house, he noticed a green sofa next to the wall and a wing chair, a radio, and a record player sitting on a rectangular wooden table next to the window, the young lady asked Chadwick if he wanted to sit down and told him he could use the telephone on the table next to the wing chair and she asked Chadwick if he wanted something to drink and he said "sure he love something hot", and she went into the kitchen and brought him out a steaming hot cup of coco, and after drinking the coco, Chadwick who had pretended to make a phone call, stood up and noticed the young lady was sitting on the couch across from where he was standing with her robe partly opened and showing some of her inner thigh and a glimpse of her pink panties, Chadwick's eyes lit amber and his retracted fangs came out as he jumped on the young lady ripping off her robe and underwear, licking her all over and her long legs while he spread them farther apart and pulling her to the floor and turned her over and now on her knees he entered her from behind hearing her grunt and scream with every thrusting motion and making hot love to her and she screamed as his fangs entered her neck from behind and at the same time of climax and with a gasp it was all over and the young lady's lifeless body was laying on the floor and Chad left the area, in a hurry and went back to their friend's house.

Chadwick also began to remember about a hunt in Chicago, he was out walking around the city and eventually go to a strip club and according to the sign outside they had partly nude girls dancing and after going into the smoke filled bar, which had red painted walls, and dim lights hanging from the ceiling, and he sat near the stage, where two girls were dancing and also touching each other and one looked to be in her early twenties and was very pretty, she had long red hair and was tall and was wearing only skimpy silk panties and she was showing off her large plump big nipped breast while the other girl had black hair, ruby red lips and she was wearing pink panties and a bra and a thigh high laced hose and was built like a brick house showing off her firm long legs and perfectly rounded ass that looked like it was busting out of her small silk panties, every time that she would bend over with her pink panties riding up, and Chadwick had a draft beer in his right hand and a cigarette in the other and the black haired lady came over to where he was sitting and asked Chadwick if she could join him and Chadwick said "sure" and he ordered the young lady a drink and after a brief introduction, the young lady put her arm around Chadwick and she seductively whispered into Chadwick's ear, while sticking in her tongue and licking his ear and asked if he wanted to take her into the backroom where they could be alone and Chadwick stood up, looked deeply into her eyes and said "I would love to" and he took her hand and the young lady led him into the back room and once they entered the room she turned and locked the door. The room was poorly lit and there was a

small bed next to a window
with the shades pulled down and
Chadwick sat on the bed and the young
lady started taking off her laced pink panties,
first pulling them down a little and pulling them back
up again and then she wiggled side to side while pulling
her silk panties completely off and kicked them toward
Chadwick, and while she was dancing in front of him very
closely, she said "do you like what you see?" and Chadwick
said "yes" and then she bent over with her laced thigh high
stockings still on, and was showing off her perfect rounded
white ass, and Chadwick could see some hair peeping through
her legs and she said "take me from behind, while she was
rubbing her fingers in her wet spot, showing Chadwick even
more of her naked body and at that time, Chadwick had his
pants down to his knees and he moved closer to her tight
bent over body and splitting her cheeks like a battering ram
he penetrated her butt and she screamed that it hurts and
then said loudly, "whip my ass", and Chadwick slapped her
tight ass cheek with his big hand while he was moving back
and forth and she kept saying "harder, harder please," and
Chadwick slapped her behind until it was red and while
hearing her pant and groan and telling him not to
stop, Chadwick rammed her so hard, that she
moved forward and hit her head on
a chair and she screamed out

as he exploded inside her hot tight body and pulled out while still dripping his male juices onto her ass, then he could feel his fangs moving out of his gums and was drooling and then his eyes lit amber and his heart was beating fast and he grabbed her shoulders from behind and bit down as his fangs entered her small neck and blood squirted, she screamed loudly and Chadwick fed on the poor young lady for about a half an hour, and then he heard a knock at the door and left the area immediately.

Chadwick later felt really bad and in tears, he cried out as to how sorry he was for what he had done and then found himself with his back to the railing of the ship sweating and in a sitting pose and then he rose up and went back to the cabin and practiced some of the exercises the Madam had shown him and then after talking with his mother about how much he loved Tracy and that he could not wait until his next meeting with the Madam in hope that one day he could start living a normal life.

CHAPTER
10 DAY TEN

September 10th 1955, Chadwick woke up at around 10 A.M. and got dressed and told his mother that Tracy and her mother would be joining them for lunch on the Lido deck today and his mother got dressed and they proceeded to the Lido deck and after they arrived, they found Tracy and her mother were already seated at a table next to a beautiful statue. Tracy was wearing pedal pushers and a plaid top and had her hair in a ponytail and Tracy and Chadwick conversed with each other and so did their mother's and Tracy said that this is the last day in South Hampton and asked Chadwick if he wanted to spend the afternoon together, Chadwick said "yes, of course" and said that they could have a tour of the engine room and the kitchen area of the ship and also join the wine tasting event and an art show on deck 5 of the ship, Tracy said that she would like that and maybe they could also play shuffleboard, after eating and planning the rest of the day, Chadwick and Tracy left for the on board tour and art show, and after playing shuffleboard they both went back to their rooms. Chadwick and his mother started getting ready for dinner, Chadwick put on gray slacks, a black shirt and a gray tie with red stripes and black winged tipped shoes while his mother wore a flowered dress. At around 5:30 P.M. They went up to the main dining room and again found Tracy and her mother were already seated. Chadwick seated his mother and sat across from Tracy who was smiling at him and said "good evening" and Chadwick responded by saying "good evening with a beaming smile" and then they all ordered dinner and talked about what a nice time they all had visiting England. Tracy asked Chadwick if he and his mother had any plans for tonight and Chadwick responded that he and his mother were going to be spending some time together after dinner knowing that he had a meeting with the Madam after dinner, but if she wanted to meet him later at their favorite spot by the smoke stack that he would be waiting for her after 11:00 P.M. Tracy had ordered a lobster tail and a salad while Chadwick ordered a rare porterhouse steak and baked potato and then they both stated how great the food was on the ship and after a little small talk at around 7:30 P.M. Chadwick and his mother left the main dining room and stopped by one of the bars to get a drink before going to see Madam Medina, Chadwick had a rum and soda and his mother had a margarita, no salt on the rocks and they conversed for a while and then Chadwick's mother went back to their room while Chadwick left to see the Madam.

After walking up to the Madam's door and knocking, Chadwick hears a gruff voice say "come in, I've been waiting for you", Chadwick entered the room, and saw the Madam was seated at the table with the black box and said please close and lock the door behind you and Chadwick did and then Chadwick sat across from the Madam, and she said in her gruff voice "have you be doing the things I told you about and practicing them?", Chadwick said "yes and he thinks they are really helping to control himself", but he still sometime finds himself wanting to hunt, but so far he has been able to control the rage inside him that wants to take over his body

and went on to say that he
and Tracy are becoming an item
and that he loves her and believes she
feels the same and knowing that helps him to
control the demon inside, the room was very dark, and
the Madam said for Chadwick to look deep into her eyes
as she started to chant, and move her hands back and forth
over the black box on the table, and Chadwick again looked
into the Madam's eyes and again it was like looking into a
window as he saw flames and smoke not unlike a volcano as
he could not move, but knew of his surroundings and she said
"I command that this beast inside this person to be gone"
and the table raised up and a green colored smoke rose up
out of the black box and at one point Chadwick heard what
sounded like thunder as the table fell back to the floor and
the Madam screamed, "Be gone, be gone I said!", and then
she chanted more and after about an hour and a half, she
stopped and snapped her fingers and turned on the lights,
and Chadwick was now able to move, but was sweating as
if he had just been running and the Madam gave Chadwick
some more mental exercises to do and told him, "not yet,
you're not cured yet, but we are making progress", and if he
does his part they can beat the thing that is trying
to take over his body and she advised him to
come back for another session on the
thirteenth and at the same time,

and advised him to practice everything she had shown him, Chadwick said he would and thanked her for everything and left at around 10:30 P.M. Chadwick stopped by he and his mother's room to give her a progress report, and then Chadwick left and started walking to go up to the smokestack deck where Tracy had been waiting, after arriving, they embraced and told each other how much they care about one another and as before they found themselves out in an out of control passion and Tracy was pulling Chadwick closer to her body while kissing and their tongues touching and they could feel the tingling and Chadwick was squeezing Tracy's tight ass through her silk panties, after putting his big hand up her red dress, Tracy was moaning and saying in her soft sexy voice that she wanted to feel Chadwick deep inside her hot body and Chadwick pulled down her red silk panties and while holding each other close, Tracy reached down with her right hand and unzipped Chadwick's pants and stuck her small hand into his pants and pulled out his already erected man tool and after both of them finished fondling each other, Tracy laid down on the floor and spread her legs wide, while opening herself up to Chadwick's big erection and she wrapped her small right hand around it and slowly moved it to her wet spot and moved the tip around the edges and with a lurch forward Chadwick could feel the penetration as he entered deep inside her hot wet body and hearing Tracy saying loudly that she loves it and not to stop while panting to every back and forth motion, after making love for about 30 minutes, they heard someone coming up the steps and they quickly composed themselves, just in time. They almost got caught by a steward who was out for a stroll and almost getting caught made it even more exciting as they left talking about how they almost got caught, walking arm in arm, Chadwick walked Tracy back to her cabin and they kissed and held each other closely and then Tracy went into her cabin while Chadwick went for a stroll around the big ship, since he was not tired. Chadwick went up to the lido deck and found himself at the bow of the ship again, it was raining lightly as he gazed out at the water and the caps were around three to four feet.

Chadwick started to remember about another time, when he was on one of his hunts on a rainy day in Chicago. It was around 1:00A.M., and he had gone for a walk about ten blocks from their residence and found a lady who looked to be in her thirties, feeding her cats on her porch at their ranch style home. She was very pretty with long black hair, and she was wearing some type of smock, white silky in color and he could see her blue panties showing through as she bent down to pour the milk into the cats bowl and he approached her and after talking for a while and introducing himself, she invited him inside and Chadwick walked into the lady's home and she asked him to sit down on the couch, which was next the window and she told Chadwick that her husband had been in the military and was killed overseas, and that she lived there alone, and never got to go out much, and she got Chadwick a steaming hot cup of coffee, and they talked for a while about each other, and after drinking a cup of hot steaming coffee, they sat on the couch for a while looking at pictures and she slowly sat closer to him and he was now looking down the top of her flimsy nightgown and saw her large firm looking breasts and then they began to kiss while feeling each other and Chadwick put his hand between her legs and began massaging her until he could feel the wetness coming through her panties and he pulled the top of her gown down exposing her big breast and he wrapped his big hand around one of them and moved his head closer and began to lick her hard nipples and she laid down on the couch and he pulled her silk panties to one side and shoved his hard man tool deep inside her as she gasped and grunted very loudly and they made loud passionate love for about an hour until Chadwick erupted like a volcano inside her and she moaned loudly with passion and Chadwick's eyes turned amber and his fangs came out and like a hungry shark he entered the lady's neck, and she screamed loudly as he sucked her blood until he was completely contempt and then left the lady who was still alive, in a flash and found himself back home, sweaty, crying and praying to God to forgive him. Chadwick came back to his sense, he was still leaning over the railing of the ship and Chadwick heard someone say "good evening lad", it was an older man who was also out for a stroll, he said it's kind of humid and Chadwick answered "yes it truly is and left. He went back to their room to practice some of the mental exercises the Madam had given him.

Meanwhile Tracy was in her room, thinking about Chadwick and how much that she loved him and wanted to tell him everything and did not want to keep any secrets from him and knowing that if she was to come to terms with her problems she needed to remember as much as possible and get it all out.

Tracy started to reminisce about a time when she was staying in her dorm room at her college, it was on a full moon night and she was sleeping and her roommate came in and woke her while getting dressed for bed. Tracy found herself thirsting for flesh and blood, knowing that her roommate was ovulating, and Tracy could not take it anymore and she got out of bed and got dressed and left to go on a hunt and she sneaked outside her dorm and walked around looking for prey and she noticed two security guards who were standing and talking, both were dressed in full dark blue uniforms and one of them had a lit cigarette in his right hand and Tracy felt herself starting to transform and stretching out of proportion, her mouth was elongated, her eyes lit yellow green, as she stretched out of her clothes and was now all covered with grayish hair and she moved at the speed of lighting and pounced on the two men, biting one of the guards in the jugular vein. Blood squirted out all over and at the same time taking down the other guard with her claws and she feasted on the both of them for about an hour and in a flash, she left the area and found herself naked in her dorm and later felt very bad for what she had done and then she stopped remembering, and she started crying thinking about her and Chadwick and hoped that now more than ever that the Madam could remove the Curse of the Werewolf.

CHAPTER 11 DAY ELEVEN

September 11th, after leaving England and getting back on the high seas, Chadwick found himself and his mother was playing Bingo in the blue room, and the cost was around $5.00 for 3 Bingo cards and it was around 1:30 P.M... and it was raining on deck. Since it would be a couple of days until they arrived in Italy, they decided to play Bingo with a chance to win $200 and have some fun doing it, after playing bingo for awhile they had fun, but never won anything, afterwards, they left the blue room and walked around the ship and went to one of the on-board shops.

Chadwick's mother bought a pair of earrings and Chadwick bought himself some cologne that was produced in France and three cigars and then they both went back to their cabin to start getting ready for dinner.

Chadwick, after bathing put on his gray striped suit and gray tie and his shiny black shoes while his mother put on a yellow skirt with a white top and put her hair up in a bun and at around 5:30 they both walked up to dinner and after Chadwick had seated his mother, Tracy came in by herself and Chadwick said "hi" and politely seated Tracy, he asked her where her mother was and Tracy responded that her mother was feeling ill and decided to stay in their cabin this evening and Chadwick noted that he hoped she would be feeling better and asked Tracy if she would like to go with him and his mother tonight to see a comedian who would be performing in the main auditorium at 8:00 P.M., and Tracy responded that she could not because she was going to be staying with her mother in their cabin, until at least 11:00P.M. or until her mother went to bed, "knowing that she has a meeting with the Madam at 8:00P.M. so she could try to get rid of the beast that was trying to take over her body," and Tracy advised Chadwick that she could meet with him at their favorite place at the smokestack deck after 11:00 P.M., and Chadwick agreed, and then they all conversed and ate and Chadwick hugged and kissed Tracy telling her that he would wait for her later on the smokestack deck.

Chadwick after kissing and hugging tracy, he and his mother left the main dining area and stopped by a coffee shop and had coffee and talked about Chadwick's problems and asked him if the Madam was being of any help and Chadwick said yes, she is very helpful, and her exercises, were very effective, and he soon hopes to be cured, but advised her that he still sometimes has the urge to hunt, but now finds it easier to control the rage inside him.

Chadwick also noted that he sometimes has dreams about his father, whom he had never seen and his mother said that it was not unusual considering everything that had happened in his life and hoped he would one day be able to live a normal life and that she hoped that everything would work out between him and Tracy and then Chadwick and his mother went to watch the show.

Once at the show they found seats that were near the front and they both found the show great because he and his mother were laughing out loud, as did almost everyone in the auditorium and at around 10:00 P.M. They both left the auditorium and headed back to their cabin. Afterwards Chadwick left he and his mother's cabin after telling her that he was going to be meeting up with Tracy and would see her later on and so his mother said "you kids have a nice time", and told Chadwick that she was tired and was going to bed.

After arriving at the smokestack deck, Chadwick found that it was still raining lightly, but not enough to have to go inside so he waited for Tracy, while watching the raindrops bouncing off of the deck and after about fifteen minutes, Chadwick heard someone coming up the steps and it was Tracy, "how's your mother?" Chadwick asked, and Tracy said that she was still a little ill, but after taking some medication, that she is feeling better, and is now asleep in their cabin.

Tracy, started putting her arms around Chadwick's neck and pulling him into her plump breast, while he was caressing her round tight ass, and while sliding his hand up her skirt fingering and squeezing her tight ass, and hearing her moan and in a panting tone saying she wants to feel him inside her tight young ass, Chadwick turned Tracy around and she bent over and Chadwick lifted her skirt and

put his big hand into her
white silk panties, pulled them
down to her knees, showing off her well
rounded, alabaster smooth ass and he pulled
out his already erect man tool and moved into her
slowly while spreading her cheeks as he penetrated her hot
body and she backed up and took everything he had while
screaming that it hurts, but do not stop, while panting in pain
and pleasure while feeling the rain drops hitting the bareness
that was exposed as they were slipping and sliding on the
wet deck, as Chadwick then pulled out of her tight butt, and
exploded all over Tracy's alabaster half-moon backside as she
screamed in pleasure and then Chadwick laid down on the wet
deck and Tracy stepped out of her silk panties, which was now
at her ankles and she straddled him like a horse as Chadwick
laid on the wet deck ready for her warm hot body and while
still on top of him, Tracy reached down and grabbed his
large man tool with her wet right hand and forced it inside
her tight wet body as she slid down taking it all, and she rode
him like a bronco and in the rain they made passionate love as
they thirsted for each other like a man in the desert thirsting
for a taste of water as Chadwick exploded deep inside her
and Tracy screamed and moaned with pleasure and
said that she loved Chadwick with all of her
heart and then it started raining more
and Chadwick and tracy after

getting fully dressed he and
Tracy walked, arm in arm back
inside, and afterwards they walked
around inside the big ship and Chadwick then
walked Tracy back to her cabin, but neither wanted to
let go but Tracy reluctantly entered her cabin.

Chadwick then left and went up to the lido deck and again found himself at the bow of the ship, and while leaning over the rails and watching the rain beat against the ship, Chadwick was watching the white caps on the water as far as one could see and like before he started thinking about another time when he was about twenty three years old and he and his mother went to a ski resort area that was out in the middle of nowhere os they could rest and relax, located in Denver, Co,. For a two week vacation and even though he nor his mother could ski they both had a great time, watching others ski and watching the snow outside while drinking hot chocolate by the indoor fireplace and at the cabin next to theirs, Chadwick noticed a beautiful blond haired lady who was vacationing with two other young ladies and every time he saw her in the snow, his eyes would start to light amber and he would start foaming at the mouth and he knew he had to have her and he noticed that every day at the same time, the other ladies would have their skis and would leave at around 1:00 P.M. and would not come back until around 5:P.M., and that she must not ski, so if he was to have her he must do it when the others were gone.

So the next day Chadwick saw like before, the other two ladies were leaving their cabin with their skis and in about twenty minutes, Chadwick went to the ladies cabin and knocked on the door and he introduced himself and the kind young lady invited him inside on this cold and snowy day and she said that her name was Billie Jo and that she was from Texas and said she was in college. She and her two friends were vacationing, but she did not ski and Chadwick told her he did not ski either and the young lady gave him a cup of hot chocolate and after drinking the coco and conversing, Chadwick started to walk out and Chadwick gave her smiling stare and the young lady as if she was in some type of a trance, said "why don't you stay", since her friends won't be back for another three hours and they have nothing else to do and Chadwick sat down beside the young lady on the leather sofa and they found themselves hugging and kissing on the couch and Billie Jo stood up and started pulling down her tight pants showing off her beautiful smooth body and was standing there in her white silk panties and her plaid shirt.

Chadwick noticed that she had a great body and she pulled down her panties and kicked them off and at that time Chadwick had his pants to his knees and he threw her onto the floor, near the fireplace and guided his large man tool as he penetrated her soft young body and she moaned and panted like a dog with every motion as they made love to each other like bears in a cave, as the fire wood crackled and the young lady screamed with pleasure, Chadwick climaxed the same time as her, and like an out of control beast, Chadwick went into a rage and his fangs came out and he foamed at the mouth and his eyes lit amber as he bit into the young lady's neck, she screamed almost in pleasure and he extracted her blood until she was left almost lifeless then like the superhuman that he is, he left as quickly as he came and went back to their cabin, not knowing if the young lady was dead or going to be turned into another vampire.

After remembering, Chadwick now found himself crying and praying, that if there is a God, to please forgive him for his misdeeds and he hated what he knew he had done and as he again found himself sitting on the deck near the bow of the ship and was sweating as if he had just ran up twelve flights of steps and reaching onto the rail he pulled himself up

to his feet and started making
his way back to their cabin and
once inside, he started practicing the
mental exercises the Madam had given him
and prayed again that if there is a God, please let me
be able to live a normal life and please let him and Tracy be
able to get married and have normal kids and to be able to
live a normal life together and then Chadwick drank a glass
of milk and went to bed.

CHAPTER
12 DAY TWELVE

September 12th 1955 The twelfth day of the cruise, Chadwick slept in his room until around noon and then he and his mother got dressed and went up to the lido deck to eat lunch, and there was a smorgasbord and they could not believe all the different types of food available, but he and his mother just had sandwiches, some soft drinks and talked some more about the show that had been performed the night before and what a great time they both were having on this cruise of a lifetime and Chadwick again told his mother that he loved Tracy with all of his heart and knew she felt the same toward him and he

found himself getting closer
to her as the days went by and his
mother said that she was glad for him
and wished him all of the best. Now the rain
had stopped and the sun was shining on the water as
far as they could see.

Chadwick's mother said that they should be arriving in Italy this evening, and she could not wait to see everything and Chadwick said yes and he hoped he and Tracy could tour Rome and Venice together because it sounded like the romantic date, and they both needed each other.

His mother said, not to forget about the Leaning Tower of Pisa, and after about 2 hours on the lido deck, Chadwick and his mother walked around the big ship and then they went back to their cabin and rested for a while and at around 4:00 P.M. They both started getting ready for dinner and it was a formal dinner so after bathing, Chadwick put on his tuxedo and a white ruffled shirt with cufflinks, and a black bow tie and cumberbun, paired with shiny black shoes and his mother put on a formal gown with laces and a double pearl necklace and earrings to match and Chadwick and his mother started walking up to the main dining room admiring the beautiful artworks on the walls, Chadwick noticed that Tracy and her mother were already seated at their table so Chadwick and his mother joined them and after seating his mother Chadwick put her shawl on the back of her chair.

Chadwick asked Tracy's mother if she was feeling better and she said "that she was feeling much better and thanked him for his concern" and Chadwick said "he was glad" and then they all ordered dinner. Chadwick ordered a bottle of white wine for the table, and after filling all of the glasses, Chadwick could not help but notice Tracy's beautiful smile as he viewed her through his sparkling wine glass and they all drank and ate and talked about being in Italy and since none of them had ever been abroad before, they were very excited and Chadwick explained that they are having another musical in the main auditorium tonight and that he and his mother are going, and asked Tracy and her mother if they wanted to join them and Tracy spoke directly and said that "she and her mother would be delighted."

At around 7:30P.M. Tracy and Chadwick left the dining room and told their mothers to save them seats in the auditorium because they would meet them there later. Tracy and Chadwick, left arm in arm, out of the main dining room and they walked up to the lido deck and toward the bow of the ship and Chadwick said that the

ocean air smells fresh and the
breeze feels good too, and Tracy
concurred as she slowly moved closer to
Chadwick and kissed him on the right cheek
and as they both watched the moonlight dancing on
the waves, they embraced and told each other how much
they loved each other, and hoped that it would never end and
then Tracy and Chadwick passionately shared a loving kiss
and left the area and stopped by one of the bars on the lido
deck and ordered two mango margaritas with a small white
and blue striped umbrella sitting on top of the glass and after
finding a table on the port side of the deck overlooking the
ocean, Chadwick pulled out a cigar from his right shirt pocket
and asked Tracy if she minded if he smoked and Tracy said
that she did not mind, and Chadwick said added he didn't
smoke much, "just a good cigar once in a while" and Tracy
said "that is alright and that she liked the aroma of a good
cigar and then Chadwick cut the end off of the Churchill size
cigar and put it to his mouth and Tracy struck a match and
lit it for him, Chadwick thanked her as he puffed and blew
smoke into the air. After Chadwick and Tracy conversed for
a while, Chadwick put out his cigar and they finished their
drinks and Chadwick and Tracy walked around
the big ship and then they went into the
auditorium to meet with their mothers
at the musical and they found

their mother's seated up next to the front of the stage and they had saved them two seats. The show was great with a Frank Sinatra look alike who sang just like him and the dancers looked as if they had come out of Hollywood or Broadway and at the end of the show everyone in the audience stood to their feet, clapping and cheering and then they all walked out together and Chadwick asked Tracy if she wanted to walk around more and she said "yes, but she did not want to stay out too late" because the ship would be ported in Italy tomorrow and she wanted to get early start seeing the beauty of Italy, early in the morning and if Chadwick was going to be touring with her, he too should turn in early and he agreed.

After walking around for a bit, Chadwick walked Tracy back to her room, and they kissed good night and hugged and then Chadwick left and walked around for a while and again found himself at the bow of the ship looking at the lights of the city glowing on the waves.

Chadwick started to reminisce about another time that he and his mother were taking a vacation in Ontario, Canada and it was during the summer, Chadwick and his mother had taken a bus to Niagara Falls and the falls were beautiful and one of the greatest natural sites either of them had ever seen, and they stayed in one of the best hotels in Canada and on the third night of their adventure, Chadwick remembered, going out at night and was walking around and he came up on a Country and Western bar and he went into the bar. Most of the guys there were wearing cowboy hats and wearing boots and jeans so Chadwick who looked somewhat out of place with what he was wearing, tan pants and a striped button up shirt and sneakers and he ordered a beer, and sat down at the bar on a stool and listened to the live country band play, and a young lady walked over to where he was and sat down next to Chadwick and Chadwick introduced himself and the lady said that her name was Charlotte Jones, she had sandy color medium length hair and was wearing cut off jean shorts, which complemented her figure and her long tan legs and she had on a plaid shirt that was tied in the front, showing off her flat stomach, and after talking for a while, Charlotte asked Chadwick if he wanted to dance, and Chadwick said "sure." He took the young cowgirl by the hand and went onto the dance floor and was dancing to some type of a Country Waltz and the lady told Chadwick that she had her truck parked outside and asked if he would like to go for a ride with her and Chadwick said "yes" and that it sounded like a lot of fun and after the music stopped, Chadwick and Charlotte left the bar and when they went outside, he noticed that she had a new 1955 truck, it was blue in color and they left in the young lady's truck and while driving around the area she told Chadwick that she was a farm girl and that she lived with her dad on a farm, located just outside the city limits and that her mother had died when she was a baby and she is somewhat of a tomboy, and Chadwick told her he thought that she was very pretty, and the young lady turned onto a dirt and gravel road that seemed to be in the middle of nowhere and came up to a big two story farmhouse with a barn nearby, Charlotte told Chadwick that her dad was asleep, but they could be alone in the cattle barn.

Charlotte and Chadwick got out of the truck and walked into the cattle barn, and it smelled terrible, but once she put her arms around him and pulled him close to her, Chadwick soon forgot about the smell and they started kissing each other and Chadwick put his forefinger up along Charlotte's smooth thigh and up into the left leg of her shorts, touching her tenderness, while she was moaning and telling him not to stop and that she wanted to feel all of him inside of her and Chadwick undid her shorts and pulled them off and then slowly pulled down her panties and started kissing and licking her all over as he laid her down on the hay in the barn and he penetrated her tender body with his manhood and they made love like a stallion on a mare and then Chadwick noticed that Charlotte's eyes lit amber and he could feel her fangs biting his neck and sucking his blood and Chadwick knew by now that she was a vampire as well and Chadwick's heart was beating faster and his eyes also lit amber and he was drooling like a sick dog and as they continued to make love in all positions and feasted on each other, until they were both satisfied and then they composed themselves and talked for a while about their circumstance. Charlotte and Chadwick got back into her truck and she took Chadwick back to his hotel and dropped him off and they saw each other the next night and the next day Chadwick and his mother left to return to their residence in Chicago.

Chadwick stopped reminiscing and found himself staring at the lights of the city that was glowing off of the ocean and he knew that he had to beat the curse of the vampire that was inside of him and then Chadwick walked back to his room for the night.

Chapter
13 Day Thirteenth

September 13, 1955, The M.S.S Goliath ported in Italy, Chadwick and his mother got up at around 10 AM. Chadwick put on his jeans and a plaid long sleeved shirt since the temperature was around 55 degrees outside and he also took a jacket with him. He and his mother walked up to the Lido deck for brunch before heading on to the shore and then they met Tracy and her mother on the star-bird side of the Lido deck at around 11am and Chadwick made a sandwich from the food bar, had a bowl of vegetable soup while his mother had a bowl of potato soup and Tracy and her mother both had vegetable

soup and toast and they all
had hot coffee and they talked
about how nice it is to be in Italy and all
agreed to take at least one tour together.

After brunch Chadwick, Tracy and their mothers went onto the shore of Italy and were all greeted by a five person Italian string band, singing some type of greeting song in Italian and it was great. Rome was different, the old buildings were beautiful but the city itself was a bit dirty in some of the areas they toured, but the beauty of the scenery prevailed over all of that and then they went into a nice restaurant and Chadwick and Tracy ordered lasagna and it was very spicy, but very tasty and they ordered a bottle of red wine for the table, the service was great and after eating, all four of them toured some more of the city and Chadwick told their mothers that he and Tracy were going to be touring Venice tomorrow and will be leaving early at around 8 am because the ship will be leaving Italy at 6pm. Both mothers said that they hoped they would have a great time and Chadwick's mother said that they would be staying on the ship and would be playing Bingo in the lounge.

Tracy and Chadwick were so excited thinking
about it, as they gazed into each other's eyes over
a glass of wine that they had purchased
from a street vendor and after

touring some of the Roman ruins and historic buildings, they all headed back to the ship.

Once back on board the ship, Chadwick and his mother went back to their cabin to relax, and after about an hour, they started getting ready for dinner, it was a casual dinner so Chadwick wore a sport coat and green trousers and a button up gray shirt and his mother put on an orange color long smock style dress and then they went up to the main dining room for dinner.

Once everyone was seated, Chadwick ordered a T-bone steak cooked rare with mashed potatoes and a bottle of red wine to be served with their meals and his mother ordered grilled chicken breast with fried rice. Tracy and her mother ordered the T-bone steak and mashed potatoes and Tracy also requested that her steak be rare. When Chadwick cut his steak and put a piece into his mouth and started chewing, it felt strange and he started to choke and he could feel his fangs moving in and out as he covered his mouth with his hands and said "there's garlic!" as he spit the steak out in his napkin and put it on his plate and excused himself from the table and left. His mother said "oh no, he is allergic to garlic!" and she also excused herself and left to go find Chadwick and Chadwick's mother found him down the hallway in a coffee shop, drinking a glass of water and his mouth was raw inside and a couple of red bumps showed up on the outside his lips and his mother consoled him and asked if he wanted to go back to the cabin and Chadwick replied that he did not and that he would go back into the dining room since he did not swallow the steak he would be alright. He and his mother went back into the dining room and found Tracy had sent back her steak because she was also allergic to garlic and had now ordered the roasted chicken. Chadwick sat back down and said that he was sorry for the mishap and Tracy explained that she understood and said she was also allergic to garlic and after Chadwick's reaction, she ordered chicken so Chadwick also ordered the roasted chicken and advised the waiter that he was allergic to garlic.

Tracy asked Chadwick if he wanted to go do something after dinner and Chadwick said he still was not feeling well after the garlic episode and thinks that he is going back to his cabin, and maybe later they could do something so after dinner Chadwick and his mother went back to their cabin, room I-999 and after Chadwick had rested for a while, he told his mother he was to meet with the Madam tonight at 8pm and then he left.

After arriving at the Madam's door Chadwick knocked and heard a gruffly voice say "come on in Chadwick, I've been expecting you," and Chadwick entered the Madam's room, which was very dark. The Madam was seated at the table with the black box in the middle and said, "sit down", and Chadwick sat down and the Madam asked if he had been practicing what she had told him earlier and Chadwick said yes and he thinks it is helping, but he had a garlic episode in the dining room earlier this evening after biting a piece of steak that was drenched in garlic, and other than a raw mouth he is alright and the Madam said she was sorry about that and hoped that it would heal and Chadwick also explained to the Madam that he was in love with Tracy Fields and the Madam said "I think she is right for you and could possibly add to your cure" and then the Madam started chanting loudly and waving her hands, palms down, back and forth over the black box in the middle of the table and said "look deep into my eyes" and Chadwick did and again it was like looking through a window and he was unable to move and looking into her eyes was like looking at a movie of his past as the Madam yelled out "you must leave this body, you beast, you are not wanted here, as she yelled, "come out" green smoke arose from the black box and the table shook with every command from the Madam and after about an hour of this type of excursion from this, the Madam snapped her fingers, and gave Chadwick more exercises to do and said he was not yet cured but believes he was making progress and said that she would see him back on the 17th at the same time.

Chadwick left the Madams cabin and went back to his cabin and once inside the cabin, his mother quizzed him about how everything went with the Madam and Chadwick said just fine and thinks he is making progress and Chadwick also told his mother he can't stop thinking about Tracy and the Madam thinks that Tracy may be playing a role in his cure his mother said that she thinks Tracy is good for him and she hopes for them the best and after a few minutes, Chadwick told his mother that he was going to find Tracy and see if she wanted to walk around the ship so Chadwick left and went to Tracy's Cabin and knocked and Tracy answered the door and said "come on in", and said her mother is at a late show and won't be back for another two hours and Chadwick entered and Tracy closed the door and locked it and said she had missed him and wanted to know how he was feeling since dinner and Chadwick said he now feels great as Tracy invited Chadwick to sit with her on her bed and after sitting on

Tracy's bed, Chadwick put his arms around Tracy and they started to kiss as he pressed his lips to hers and their tongues tingled as they touched and Tracy said that she wanted to feel all of Chadwick inside of her and he felt her plump breast with his left hand while putting his other hand between her legs and rubbing her soft tender skin under her silk panties and Tracy pulled off her panties and got onto his lap and Chadwick penetrated her tight body as Tracy gasped and groaned and was panting while riding him and like an out of control wildebeest, they made passionate love for about twenty minutes, and then composed themselves and later Tracy's mother came back and started getting ready for bed and Chadwick said he had better leave since they had to be up early in the morning to tour Venice and Chadwick sweetly kissed and held Tracy tightly, pulling her closer to his body, and told her how much he loved her and needed her in his life and as Tracy gazed into Chadwick's eyes, she said that she loved him more than life, and hope that they would always be together and Chadwick said that he felt the same and said that they have a lot in common, and he believes that they were definitely meant for each other.

After kissing and hugging each other and saying their goodbyes,

Chadwick reluctantly, left Tracy's room and walked up to the Lido Deck and walked around the ship for a while and ended up back in the casino and he put in a few dollars and coins and won a small jackpot of about fifty dollars and he cashed out. The young lady in the cashier's cage told Chadwick that she had been watching him play for a while and said that her name was, Hellan Wilcox and went on to say that she was from London England, "her English accent was piercing and Chadwick liked hearing her speak", and she said that she had been working on the cruise ship for about four years and she said that she thought Chadwick was a good looking man and asked if he had a girlfriend, as her brown eyes glistened in the low light, Chadwick told her that he had met a young lady while on the cruise, and that they have been seeing each other every day, and Hellan told Chadwick that if they break up to come and see her, and if he wants to come and visit her anyway she did not mind as well and said that her cabin was on the lower deck in room L-119 and she smiled, licked her lips and she went on to say if Chadwick needed anything, to just stop by the casino and talk to her and that she is not working on the fourteenth and that was her day off and Chadwick said alright and even though he could feel his fangs moving in and out, he could

only think of Tracy and how
much he really loved her and then
thanked the young lady and composed
himself to leave the casino and then he went
back to his cabin, I-999 and practiced some of the
excises the Madam had given him, and afterwards he went
to bed, thinking about how much he loved Tracy and how
excited he was about seeing Venice with her tomorrow and
how romantic it was going to be for the both of them.

CHAPTER
14 DAY FOURTEEN

September 14, 1955, the fourteenth day of the cruise, Chadwick woke up at 6 AM and thinks about the day he will spend with the one he loves, he starts getting ready by putting on his brown pants and a pullover shirt and sneakers, and kissed his mother goodbye and then went to meet with Tracy on the lido deck, Once on the lido deck he went to the breakfast bar and took two pieces of toast and some bacon and poured himself a cup of hot coffee and added a little cream and found a table on the dock side of the ship. Tracy came by to where he was and she looked beautiful wearing knee length white pants that hugged her body like a second skin veiling a blue flowered long sleeved blouse which accented her beautiful upper body and complexion, Tracy had an orange juice and coffee and a bowl with fresh fruit and came over and sat across Chadwick and said "Good morning," Chadwick said "Good morning gorgeous", and they both ate and after some small talk, they went to the gangway and walked off the ship to take their tour through Florence and then on to Venice, the old structures were breathtaking as they went through Florence and the scenic side was beautiful and Chadwick and Tracy had a ball and once in Venice they toured the canals in a gondola while listing to the gondolier sing an Italian love song and later had their picture taken while holding and kissing each other while on the ride. The gondolier was great and sang while taking them through the canals, afterwards they stopped at a restaurant and ate a snack before heading back to the dock. Chadwick was feeling so good knowing he had met someone who really cared about him and knew he wanted to spend the rest of his life with Tracy, but also in the back of his mind he knew he had to first beat the beast that is still trying to take over his life. Tracy felt the same way, but knew that being with Chadwick has been very helpful with her hidden problem and also knew she had to defeat the wolf

that is trying to take over her
life as well and thought of how
she can share that part of her life with
Chadwick and worried that he would not
understand, "how could he? how could any normal
person understand", saying to herself she does not want to
be a freak, but only wants to live a happy and normal life with
Chadwick and also thinking that she has a meeting with
Madam tonight. Chadwick told Tracy that its black tie event
tonight so they had to dress up, Tracy told Chadwick that she
would be at dinner but had to spend some time with her
mother after dinner, (knowing that she had a meeting with
the Madam) Chadwick said okay and that he and his mother
would go to a show after dinner so could they meet up later
at the smokestack deck and Tracy said fine, make it at around
11 PM. Chadwick said that sounded great and he could not
wait as he ran his fingers through her beautiful hair and
touched her face, and they started back to the big ship. After
they went back on the ship Chadwick walked Tracy back to
her room and kissed and hugged her and then went back to
his cabin to get ready for the night, Chadwick was tired but
very happy and his mother asked if they had fun touring
Italy, Chadwick said that it was the best time of his
life and went on to say he loved Tracy and
they have so much in common and he
enjoys every minute and second

he gets to spend with her and he also told his mother that Tracy would be at dinner tonight but afterwards she would be spending time with her mother until around 11PM tonight and Chadwick asked his mother if she wanted to go to a show and pointed out that the same comedian would be performing at 8 PM, his mother said "sure". At around 4:30 PM. Chadwick put on his black tuxedo and black bow tie and cumberbun and black shining shoes and his mother wore a black sparkling long gown with her hair in a bun and a pearl necklace (they looked fit to dine with a king) after getting ready for dinner Chadwick and his mother headed up to the main dining room and when they arrived, Tracy and her mother were already seated, Chadwick seated his mother and sat across from Tracy, who looked stunning in her sparkling blue knee length dress and was wearing a choker and shining diamond earrings and after talking and eating a scrumptious gourmet meal and drinking a couple glasses of red wine, and toasting to his mother and Tracy and her mother, Chadwick kissed and hugged tracy goodbye, and he and his mother left the dining room and stopped by the coffee shop nearby and had a cup of coffee with a little cream and his mother had green tea and they conversed about what a wonderful time they were both having on the big ship and Chadwick pulled out a cigar and cut the end off of the Churchill size cigar and lit it with a match, Chadwick held the cigar sideways across his nose while smelling the wonderful aroma as the cigar burned and after about twenty minutes in the coffee shop, Chadwick put out his cigar and he and his mother left and went to the show, once seated in the middle of the room, they found that it was very funny, even funnier than the last show, everyone laughed out loud and clapped for the comedian, afterwards Chad walked his mother back to their cabin, and Chadwick rested awhile and then at around 10:45 PM he left he and his mother's cabin and headed up to the smokestack deck to meet with Tracy, and when Chadwick arrived he found Tracy at the rail of the big ship and looking into the dark water alongside of the ship and they could see the lights of Italy as the ship moved farther away, Tracy noticed Chadwick and said "this is a beautiful night" Chadwick agreed and stated that she made the night look even more beautiful standing alongside of the rail, with her sparkling blue dress shining and the night light gleaming off of her brown eyes and then Tracy put her arms around Chadwick and pulled him close to her body and said she loved him and thinks she is very lucky to have met him and Chadwick said no, and that he was lucky one to even be in the presence of someone so pretty and nice with a wonderful personality and they again embraced and kissed and then Tracy got down on her knees and started to unzip Chadwick's pants and she reached in and pulled out his large partly erected man tool and while holding it in both of her small hands, she put it into her mouth until he was fully erected and after swirling and raking her teeth until he was ready and then she pulled it out of her mouth and still holding his man tool, in her small hand, she said now she wanted to feel him deep inside her body and she laid down on the wooden deck while pulling Chadwick on top of her and with her right hand she pulled her whie panties aside forced him inside her tight wet wanting body while panting and groaning and moaning for more and they again made passionate love until Chadwick erupted like Mount Saint Hellion's inside her hot sweating body, filling her full of his hot love and she screamed with passion and said how much she loved him and after holding each other for about an hour they left the smoke stack area arm in arm and Chadwick walked Tracy back to her cabin where they held each other and kissed more and then Chadwick left her cabin and went up to the lido deck and again found himself at the bow of the ship, looking into the dark water and was thinking about a time when he was in Chicago in the summertime. He noticed

a young lady who lived in an
apartment complex while he was
out for a long walk, he remembered how
pretty she was with long brown hair and how
he spoke to her as she was sweeping the little porch on
her apartment, she smiled and said her name was Candace
but most people call her Candy, Chadwick introduced himself
and after talking for a while, Candy invited him to come
inside her apartment, and her eyes looked like she was in some
type of a trance, Chadwick went into the young lady's
residence and she got them both a beer from the refrigerator
and poured it into two tall glasses and after about twenty
minutes they started to dance together to a slow song on the
record player and then they made passionate steamy love and
as Chadwick's heart was throbbing, his eyes lit amber and like
a viper his fangs came out and he started to inject them into
the young lady's neck when he heard the front door of the
apartment squeak and open and a big burly man who looked
like a construction worker came in, he looked to be about six
foot four and weighed about 265 lbs. He was wearing old
jeans, black boots and a leather jacket and he yelled "get away
from my wife", as he grabbed Chadwick and threw him
into the wall of the small apartment and Chadwick
now with a hurt back slid down the wall onto
the floor and thinking fast he saw a
leather tool pouch on the floor

next to the closet and picked
up a claw hammer and as the
man came closer to him he hit the man
as hard as he could in the groin with the claw
side of the hammer and he remembered the man
falling like a tree that had been cut down and while the man
was lying on the floor grabbing himself and moaning and
yelling, and he wife also yelling and screaming, Chadwick
grabbed his clothes and left like a bolt of lightning and it was
then Chadwick found out he had the ability to move faster
than sound.

After that ordeal, Chadwick then went home and it was a
while before he ventured back out again.

Not everything Chadwick did was bad, when he was
using his special vampire powers, and they did not always
involve killing or turning someone innocent into a vampire,
Chadwick remembered that one day while he and his mother
went shopping at a huge shopping center, he and his mother
had just got out of a cab at the shopping center that was
located just out of Chicago city limits and they saw a woman
who was walking with her right hand holding on to a young
boy's left hand hand and she was about to cross the
street and after stepping off of the sidewalk
and into the two lane street, Chadwick
heard a loud truck roaring

around a blind turn and saw that it was headed straight toward the unsuspecting lady and her son, Chadwick, in a flash went into the street and grabbed them both and set them safely onto the sidewalk unharmed, the lady was very thankful and said that she had never saw anyone move that quickly, and wanted to know his name, Chadwick lied and told her his name was Ralph Smite and was from out of town and very slowly walked away and then left with his mother to go shopping.

Chadwick remembered another time when he was around twenty years old, he was walking about ten blocks from his residence and he noticed fire and smoke coming from a two story house and saw someone raise a window, it was an elderly lady and her husband who was yelling for help and like lighting he ran into the smoke filled residence and went past the fire and smoke and grabbed them both and brought them outside, the man had some burns on his arm and the lady was coughing, but both were safe thanks to a hero who would never be recognized by choice, he heard sirens, and left the area in a hurry, "knowing the authorities would be asking lots of questions" so he went home.

Now after Chadwick stopped remembering he again found himself sitting with his back to the rail on the bow of the ship and he was in tears saying "he just wanted to be normal please, if there is a god, then let him be normal, and live a normal life", so he composed himself and went back to the cabin and practiced some of the exercises the Madam had shown him and said good night to his mother. He was thinking of the great times he and Tracy have been having on the ship and how much that he loves her and could hardly wait until he can see her again. He thought about how he wanted things to work out for them, and then he got ready for bed and went to sleep.

CHAPTER
15 DAY FIFTEEN

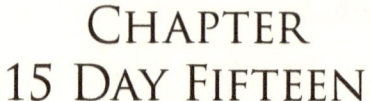

September 15, 1955 on this day at sea, Chadwick slept until around 1 PM. after waking and getting dressed, He and his mother went up to the main dining room for lunch and Chadwick had a burger and his mother had vegetable soup and they both had coffee and his mother talked about how great the show was last night and Chadwick agreed and she went on to say as to what they might do tonight, since they were not ported anywhere, Chadwick advised his mother that there was a song and dance show tonight and some live entertainment in the gold room with a live band and thinks he and Tracy might go to the gold room where the live band was playing, his mother thought that would be great and said that the theme for tonight was casual. After eating lunch Chadwick and his mother went up to the lido deck, it was a sunny afternoon so Chadwick put on his sunglasses and they walked around and looked at the beautiful water and admired the large ship and his mother noted that this is more like a floating city and she felt like royalty because it was like a dream, Chadwick agreed, Chadwick and his mother then went to a wine tasting event located at the Piano Bar and as they tasted the different types of fine wine, a man sat and played at the piano, it was great and added even more to their surroundings. After the wine tour Chadwick walked his mother back to their room where they both relaxed for about two and a half hours and then they both started getting ready for dinner, after getting ready they then headed up to the main dining room. Once there they noticed Tracy and her mother were already there, they both said hi and Chadwick after seating his mother, sat across from Tracy and she again looked fantastic in a flowered knee length dress and as she looked into Chadwick's eyes, she asked him how his day was and Chadwick had explained that he and his mother had a great day and both slept until around 1 PM and then they went to lunch at

the main dining room and
later went to a wine tasting event.

Tracy said she was glad and went on
to say that she had ordered a bottle of white wine
for dinner and Chadwick said that's great and he ordered
the flounder and a rice entree and carrot cake for dessert
and coffee and his mother also ordered the flounder and
Chadwick asked Tracy if she wanted to go to the gold room
where a big band was playing after dinner and Tracy said that
she would be delighted as they gazed into each other's eyes
and toasted to a great evening together and started sipping
their white wine as they gazed more into each other's eyes
knowing they would be going back to the smokestack deck
before going to the gold room and Chadwick could hardly
wait until dinner was over so he and Tracy could spend some
time alone and after dinner Chadwick and Tracy said goodbye
to their mothers and left the main dining room arm in arm
and then headed up to the smokestack deck and after arriving
there, they noticed another couple making love in the same
place they always meet so they left the area and Tracy said
that her Mom is going to the song and dance show tonight
and she and Chadwick can go to her room since her
mother would be gone and so Chadwick walked
Tracy to her room and said "this is even
better, not having to worry about

being caught by one of the
crew members or passengers on
the ship", and after entering the room,
Tracy put her arms around Chadwick's neck
and pulled him close to her body and he could feel her
plump breast pressing against his chest as they started to kiss
and undress each other, Chadwick threw Tracy's partly nude
body onto her bed and slowly put his big fingers inside her silk
panties and ripped them off of her smooth soft body and he
moved slowly to her toes and started kissing and licking her
smooth legs while working his way up between her smooth
thighs as she was moaning and panting, she screamed with
undying pleasure and they made love like two sweaty dingo's
in-heat and after about an hour, they composed themselves
and walked up to the gold room and danced to the music
from the live band and held each other and kissed for the rest
of the evening and afterwards Chadwick walked Tracy back
to her room where they again told each other how much they
loved one another and hoped it would never end and then
Chadwick said good night and left and as Chadwick left he
could still smell Tracy's perfume on his collar as he walked
up to the lido deck.

Chadwick found himself again on the lido
deck at the bow of the ship leaning over
and gazing into the dark water and

remembered about a time he was on a hunt back in Chicago, it was a spring time evening and he went for a walk and found himself about ten blocks from his residence and while passing a two story brick house with white shutters he noticed two young lady's taking some groceries from their old gray car and one of them dropped a bag just as he was passing by and he offered to help and started picking up a bottle of soda and some other canned food putting them back into their bag and the young lady said, "thank you" and asked him his name and Chadwick introduced himself and the young lady said her name was Nancy and she and her friend Shanna lived together in the brick house. They invited him to come inside and once inside, he remembered that the house was very nice with a big mantle and fireplace and Nancy told Chadwick that she and Shanna have lived there together for about two years and they both worked as store clerks at a supermarket nearby. Nancy and Shanna was in their early 20's, Nancy had long blonde hair, and Shanna had short brown hair and both had great figures and after telling both ladies a little bit about himself, the ladies told Chadwick a little more about themselves, Nancy asked if Chadwick wanted some wine and Chadwick said yes and the ladies went into the kitchen and came back with a bottle of wine and three

wine glasses and Chadwick
agreed to pour the wine and they
drank the whole bottle and they asked
Chadwick if he liked to dance and Chadwick
said yes, but he was not very good and Shanna put on a
record and turned down the lights and Chadwick and Nancy
started to dance then Shanna ask Chadwick if he wanted to see
her and Nancy dance together and Chadwick said that would
be great and Nancy and Shanna started to dance very closely
and was grabbing each other's behind and breast, and Nancy
asked Chadwick if he liked that and Chadwick said that he
liked it very much and the two ladies started doing nasty
things to each other while half-dressed and while panting and
moaning very loudly, Nancy grabbed Chadwick's hand and
pulled him off the couch and said "come on dance with us",
Chadwick found himself between the two young ladies who
were grabbing him and kissing him as well as each other and
the next thing Chadwick knew was that he was naked and so
were the two ladies and after making love in various positions
to both ladies on the couch and the floor, he was doing one
lady from behind while she was bent over and while she had
her head in the other girls crotch area and both panting
like dogs and drooling then he noticed the ladies
starting to bite each other on the neck and
blood was squirting everywhere and
both of their faces looked like

they had just came out of a
butcher's shop, and it was then
Chadwick knew he was in the room
with two good looking female vampires and
Chadwick's fangs came out and his eyes lit amber and
Chadwick who had thirsted for new blood like a starving
man at a buffet table, Chadwick feasted on both of them until
he was completely satisfied and both females kept moaning
and groaning and then the ladies made love with each other
and was kissing and licking each other and was lapping
blood like a cat drinking warm cream and then Chadwick
remembered leaving the young ladies at the height of their
climax.

Chadwick remembered another time while on a hunt on
one late Saturday night while going for a stroll on the beach
and while he and his mother was on vacation, he was walking
in the sand and watching the night ocean waves hitting the
beach, he came up on a young lady who was crying and
sitting on a towel, she had long reddish hair and was wearing
what appeared to be some type of white silky colored night
shorts which showed off her smooth longs legs and she was
by herself and Chadwick spoke to her and she asked
him to sit down and Chadwick told the lady his
name was Chadwick and the young lady
said her name was Rebecca but

everyone calls her Becky and Chadwick asked the young lady why she was crying and she explained that she and her boyfriend had broken up after finding out he had been with another woman and went on to say they had been together for about two years, Chadwick told the lady he was sorry to hear that and told her he was a single man and was at the beach on vacation with his mother and he lied and said he was going to college to study to be an accountant, the young lady said she and her and her family were also on vacation at the beach and told Chadwick she was also a student and was studying to be a nurse because she liked helping people and after talking for a while the young lady asked Chadwick to put his arms around her and asked if he would hold her and Chadwick put his arms around Becky and pulled her close to his body and after gazing at the night sky for a while, Becky looked into Chadwick's eyes and their lips touched lightly and then became more passionate as Chadwick could feel her tongue tingling inside his mouth and at the same time feeling her soft hand undoing his pants while laying on the sand she rolled over on top of him and moved her loose silky shorts to one side and took Chadwick's manhood into her hand and forced it into her tight skinny body and while moaning and panting like a raging bull, they made love for about half an hour, but it seemed like three and then Chadwick rolled the lady over and started kissing her between the legs as he moved over the silky shorts and put his finger inside her and she moaned and groaned and was panting as she begged him not to stop and then he started licking her as she was moving side to side with her legs spread wide and Chadwick's eyes started to glow amber and his fangs came out and he bit her between the legs, blood erupted like a freshly tapped oil well and she started to scream, first with pleasure and then in pain, as she was screaming and kicking, Chadwick had sucked more blood, as he feasted on her young body and sucked all of the life out of the young lady and left her blood stained body lying on the beach as he went back to he and his mother's hotel room and later felt bad and cried about what he had done.

Chadwick now awakened, found himself at the bow of the ship in tears as he knew he had to beat this beast that was trying to take over his life and then he heard a voice say "Are you alright sir?". Chadwick responded "yes, thank you" as the crew member walked past him, then he left and he headed back to his cabin.

Chadwick found his mother was waiting up for him and they talked about his problem and Chadwick

explained to her that he was
dealing with it, and so far he was
able to control himself and was hopeful,
that with a few more sessions with the Madam,
he thinks he will be able to control the beast that has
been dominating his life, and then they both turned in for
the night....

Chapter
16 Day sixteen

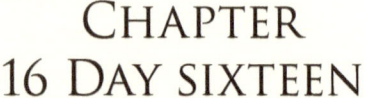

September 16th Now with the ship ported in France, Chadwick and his mother were up at around 11 AM and they were deciding what to do and Chadwick suggested that they accompany Tracy and her mother to tour France together since they would only be there for one day. They decided to meet with Tracy and her mother on the Lido Deck at noon for lunch before leaving the ship so after getting dressed Chadwick and his mother walked up to the Lido Deck and met Tracy and her Mother and sat down at a table on the open deck where they could see France while they ate lunch, Tracy looked gorgeous in a knee length gray pin striped skirt and a blue ribbon in her hair and her face glowed like the morning sun coming up on the water, Chadwick had a sandwich and vegetable soup and coffee and his mother had the same, Tracy and her mother had chicken noodle soup and coffee and they all talked about the wonderful time they were having in Europe and on the M.S.S Goliath the largest ship in the fleet, and after some more small talk, they all left the ship to tour France, their first stop was to go the Eiffel Tower, they were all amazed by how tall it was and beautiful it was, Tracy had her mother take a photo of her and Chadwick standing and holding each other in the tower and they had asked some passerby take a picture of all of them together, he was a Chinese man who was also on vacation and he name was Chang Lei and Chadwick returned the favor and used his camera to take his photo by the tower, it was a great day then they all went into Paris and had a coffee at a sidewalk cafe with umbrellas and red checked table cloths and since none of them spoke French they just ordered coffee. The old buildings were magnificent and made a great background for a good romantic atmosphere for Chadwick and Tracy as they walked arm in arm and occasionally kissing and hugging each other, Tracy explained that she was having the time of her life and

hoped it would never end and
Chadwick agreed, After touring
some more at around three PM they
all went back to the ship since it was time to
depart France at five PM, once on the ship Chadwick
and his mother went back to their cabin for rest of the
evening, his mother again said she was glad he had met Tracy
and she seemed like a nice person and she hoped the best
for them, after about two hours Chadwick and his mother
started getting ready for dinner. It was a dress casual night so
Chadwick put on his blue pants and wore a gray button up
shirt with one button opened at the collar and a checkered
jacket while his mother wore a striped dress and let her hair
hang down and at around five thirty PM they started walking
up to dinner and on the way there in the hallway was the
young girl that Chadwick was with a few nights ago, she
just smiled and said hi, and asked how his vacation was and
as Chadwick smiled at the young lady she explained maybe
they could get together again and Chadwick just nodded
and kept on walking with his mother and when they walked
up a couple of floors his mother said "Chadwick! You were
with that girl the other night!", Chadwick said "just for a
while she couldn't get her cabin door opened and
I helped, that's all it was" and I don't want
to discuss it anymore and they went
to the dining room for dinner,

after Chadwick seated his
mother Tracy and her mother
came in and Tracy looked stunning
sporting a green checked skirt and wearing a
tight white cotton blouse and jacket, Chad seated both
of them and the waiter came over and after everyone ordered
Chadwick asked the waiter to bring out a bottle of Champagne
to be served with their meal and in about ten minutes the
waiter showed up with a decanter of Champagne chilled to
perfection and served the ladies and Chadwick. Chadwick
proposed a toast, "to the great time were are having and to the
greats times to come" and they all toasted and started sipping
their drinks, afterwards Chadwick asked Tracy if she wanted
to stroll around the ship and she answered she could not
because she promised her mother she would spend some time
with her in the early evening knowing she had a date with the
madam tonight and went on to say that she would meet him
at the smokestack deck an around eleven PM if that would
be alright with him and Chadwick agreed so Chadwick and
his mother left the main dining room after eating, and was
wandering around the ship and stopped at a coffee shop and
Chadwick had cappuccino and his mother had coffee with
cream, Chadwick pulled out a Churchill size cigar
and cut off the end and put it in his mouth
and lit it with a match and he and
his mother conversed about the

great time they were having
and what a nice night for a
stroll it was, while on the outer deck of
the ship and after they finished their drinks,
Chadwick and his mother went to the outside deck
for a stroll, the stars were bright and the breeze felt good, his
mother explained that this was the kind of life she had always
wanted for Chad, after they walked for a while Chadwick
and his mother went back inside and caught the last part of
the comic show, it was very entertaining and they both left
the show still laughing as they headed back to their room
and after resting in the room for about two hours Chadwick
told his mother he was to meet with Tracy at eleven o'clock
and his mother said it is only ten thirty now and Chadwick
said "I'll be waiting for her at the SmokeStack Deck" and he
left. after leaving his room he noticed a door open up in the
hallway, it was the lady he had helped with her locked door,
she said hi and Chadwick spoke and she invited him in to
her cabin, Chadwick knowing he was to meet with Tracy said
he was not feeling well and was headed to see the medic for
some medication for his upset stomach and left the young
lady. After arriving at the SmokeStack Deck Chadwick
leaned over the rail and looked deep into the water
thinking about how much he loved Tracy and
what a life they could have together
if he could only beat the rage

inside him and he squeezed the rail tightly and prayed that he would be cured and said "If there is a god please cure me please, please." and then he heard someone coming up the steps and it was Tracy and she said "so you have been waiting for me!" Chadwick said yes and that he had been thinking of her ever since they parted ways earlier, Tracy concurred and put her arms around Chadwick's neck and looked into his eyes and kissed him and as they tasted each other while grabbing and touching each other Chadwick turned Tracy around and she grabbed the ship's rail with both hands and he lifted her skirt and pulled her pink silk panties down to her knees exposing her alabaster tight behind and he could hear her panting as he penetrated her tight young behind, and Tracy was moaning and groaning and said in her soft voice for Chadwick not to stop as they made passionate love for about a half an hour, like two dingo's in heat until they both were completely sissified.

Afterwards, they embraced and composed themselves and left walking arm in arm and held hands while admiring the ship and the lovely starry night as the water seemed to glisten as they could feel the warm and cool breeze as they strolled, later Chadwick walked Tracy back to her room and again they embraced, hugged and kissed and explained that they

never wanted to be apart and
then Chadwick left and went
back to their room and his mother was
awake and asked if he had a good time with
Tracy, Chadwick said "yes we enjoyed the stars and
beautiful night air", Chadwick's mom told Chadwick he
had better get some sleep since it was so late, He agreed and
said that he will after he does some of the madam's excises.
Afterwards Chadwick went to sleep.

CHAPTER
17 DAY 17

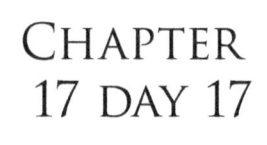

September 17th 1955, at around noon Chadwick's mother woke him and he started getting ready for the day, he put on tan pants and a polo shirt paired with sneakers and his mother wore a sundress she had bought earlier from the islands and then they went up to the Lido Deck to eat lunch, Chadwick had a hamburger, potatoes, a slice of melon and orange juice while his mother had a fruit salad, coffee and wheat toast with butter,. His mother said there is an another art show at two o'clock and asked if he wanted to go, Chadwick said yes since we are out to sea and it was overcast and looked like it could possibly rain after they ate lunch, Chadwick and his mother started walking toward the red room where there was an art show going on, the art show was great they served champagne and had scrumptious snacks, the art was beholding to the eye because the colors were perfect and blended perfectly so his mother bought another painting of a sea scape to be hung in their hallway when they get home, his mother added as they were leaving that Chadwick had to meet with the Madam tonight, Chadwick said he knew that and believed she was helping him fight and beat the demon inside him, his mother said she felt like it was all her fault and if she had only known his dad was a vampire she would not have been with him but added that she would not have a good loving son such as him but in some ways she still feels bad, They went back to their room to rest up for the evening festivities and at around five o'clock they started getting ready for dinner, it was a formal night so Chadwick put on his black pants, a white ruffled button up shirt and a black bow tie and a white dinner jacket with silk lapels paired with shiny black shoes and his mother wore a long gown and pearls and wore her hair in a bun, after getting ready they both started walking towards the dining room and once in the main dining room they noticed Tracy and her mother were already seated, Tracy laughed and said "what took you so long?" and Chadwick said they were sleeping and got up later than usual as he seated his mother, Chadwick advised Tracy that he and his mother would be spending time together after dinner and they could meet later at their usual spot at around eleven o'clock, knowing he had a meeting with the madam after dinner so after eating a king's meal and drinking red wine, Chadwick and his mother left and headed to his mother's room and after resting a while Chadwick headed up to see the Madam, once outside her room he knocked on the door and a gruffly voice said "come on in I've been expecting you," Chadwick walked into the dark room where the Madam was sitting and she asked how things were going, Chadwick replied that things were great and that he and Tracy were getting closer by the day and so far by using her exercises he had been able to control the rage inside him, like before she waved her palms over the black box sitting in the middle of the table and chanted something, it sounded like Arabic but he had no idea what she was chanting and again she yelled for Chadwick to peer deeply into her eyes and like looking into dark windows Chadwick could not move and felt helpless as green smoke started coming out of the black box and he felt like he was floating as the table shook and

the madam kept yelling for
the monster inside him to come
out! After about an hour and a half the
madam snapped her fingers and Chadwick felt
he was back in control of his body and the madam
then turned on the lights and said that she would need one
more session with him on the 20th at around ten o'clock and
wished him well and gave him some more pointers and then
Chadwick left her room and headed up to the SmokeStack
Deck where he hoped to find Tracy and after arriving at the
SmokeStack deck he found that Tracy had been waiting for
him and they embraced and looked deep into each other's
eyes and both exclaimed how they had missed each other
and could not wait to see each other and after kissing and
caressing each other Tracy asked Chadwick if he wanted
to walk around the ship and he said yes so they left the
SmokeStack Deck since there were other people coming up
the steps, and so they walked holding hands and kissing
and admiring each other and Chadwick telling Tracy that
she smells like a freshly picked rose and then Chadwick and
Tracy then found themselves in a bar two decks down and
Tracy ordered a mild fruit drink while Chadwick ordered
a beer and pulled out a Churchill size cigar and cut
off the end and put it between his lips and
again Tracy wanted to light it and she
struck a match and held it to

Chadwick's Cigar and Tracy shared with Chadwick that she often thinks of her father whom she had never seen and wonders what he was like knowing that he had been a full-fledged Werewolf and maybe how her life would be different if he were alive and noted that sometimes in a weird way she missed him and cries when thinking about him and Chadwick told Tracy that they have so much in common and that he too thinks of his father and what it would be like to have had a dad in his life knowing that his real dad was a vampire and murderer.

Chadwick finished his beer and Tracy finished her drink and they left the bar arm in arm and walked to the bow of the ship and Chadwick explained to Tracy that he sometimes comes to the bow of the ship to look at the ocean, and he finds himself thinking about his past and also his future with her.

While Chadwick was looking out over the ocean waters and listening to the wave caps hitting the ship, Chadwick was feeling Tracy's breath in his ear while he was looking way out into the ocean, near what seemed to be the ocean's end, Chadwick and Tracy saw a small light, and it was another ship's beacon shining in the water and they both conversed as to what kind of ship it might be, and maybe another cruise or possibly a military ship and after talking and walking for a while they notice on the starboard side of the ship, a shooting star crossing the sky lighting up the water and "Chadwick made a wish which he kept to himself" and they both said that this was a good sign as they watch it disappeared into the sea and then Chadwick started walking with Tracy back to her room and once at the room Chadwick told Tracy he really loves her a lot and misses her when she isn't near, while Tracy was holding Chadwick so close they were almost like one body, Tracy told Chadwick that she was so glad she had met him and hoped their relationship would flourish and that she knew she was in love with him and that one day, maybe they would marry, knowing that she had to first beat the raging mad bull inside her.

Chadwick said he hoped for the same and loved her more than life itself and then they kissed good night and Chadwick left and walked back to his cabin.

Once back at the Cabin, his mother was still awake and wanted to know about his visit with the Madam and wanted to know how everything went and Chadwick said it was great and that she wanted to see him one more time on the 20th at ten o'clock and Chadwick also noted that he loved Tracy and that she feels the same about him and

one day he hoped to marry
her and possibly have a family
of his own and his mother wished he
and Tracy the best and said that it would be
nice but they better go to bed for now and Chadwick
agreed.

CHAPTER 18

September 18th 1955, On the high seas in the Atlantic Ocean, Chadwick slept until about one o'clock and he and his mother got dressed and walked up to the Lido Deck to eat a late lunch and the water was a little rough and the white caps were high at around 6 to 7 foot waves and it was a little cool on the Lido Deck, but the white caps were beautiful to watch as they slammed against the sides of the ship, which was traveling about 20 knots while cutting through the rough sea and after eating lunch, Chadwick and his mother left the Lido Deck and went to meet with Tracy and her mother for a game of shuffleboard that was held on the Atrium Deck, Tracy was wearing blue jean knee knockers paired with sneakers and her hair was tied back in a ponytail and they played shuffle board for about an hour and a half and Chadwick and tracy played against their mothers, and they won one game and their mothers won the other 3 games, then Chadwick and Tracy hugged and kissed and they went their separate ways.

Chadwick walked his mother back to their room and they rested and relaxed for about half an hour and at around four thirty PM, Chadwick and his mother started getting ready for dinner and Chadwick put on his black suit and white shirt and a black tie and his black buckle up shoes and his mother put on a white skirt with a blue blouse and after getting ready, they both started walking up the steps to go to dinner and after entering the main dining room, Chadwick seated his mother. After a little while, Tracy and her mother came in and Chadwick seated them both and sat down while placing the white cloth napkin on his lap, Chadwick looked deeply into Tracy's eyes and started talking about what fun they all had while playing shuffleboard and Tracy's mom concluded that she has been having a ball on the cruise and knows it won't be her last cruise, and that she and Tracy were having the time of their lives and hated the thought of it ending and

Chadwick and his mother
agreed and Chadwick's mother
told Tracy and her mother about a
dance tonight in the green room with a live
band, playing some kind of new music called rock
and roll and asked if they wanted to go and check it out and
Tracy and Chadwick agreed they would love to and after
they had eaten dinner and had their deserts, they all left with
Chadwick and Tracy arm in arm and their mothers not far
behind them, and after arriving at the green room they found
the music was really loud, a new boogie type music, Tracy
and Chadwick went onto the dance floor and were dancing to
the new sound, Tracy explained that this is great, Chadwick
was also intrigued and after dancing to a fast sounding song
to what they called the boogie, the music slowed down and
they began to slow dance closely and Tracy's head was on
Chadwick's shoulder and he could smell her perfume as he
whispered into her ear as to how much he cared for her and
wanted her now, and wanted to feel himself himself inside
her warm tight body and Tracy moaned lightly pulling him
even closer to her body and then the music stopped playing
and Chadwick asked Tracy if she wanted to go to their
room since their mothers were having fun here,
Tracy agreed so they told their mothers they
were going for a walk and left arm in
arm as they walked to Tracy's

room, and once in the room Chadwick threw Tracy onto the bed and put both of his hands up her skirt, Tracy groaned loudly and then he pulled off her silky white panties and started kissing her toes working his way up to her smooth thighs and with his big hands he gently parted her tender skin while licking as far inside her wet body as his tongue could reach while Tracy was moaning and yelling and panting short breaths saying "please don't stop, don't stop oh my god don't stop" and then she gasped and pulled Chadwick on top of her yearning hot body saying she wanted all of him inside her and like a raging bull he entered her soft tight body while both were sweating and groaning and moaning as they made love for about an hour until he exploded deep inside her and they held each other tight for a while and made up the messed bed and left her room arm in arm before his mother came back and then they went back to the Lido Deck to get a snack from the late night food bar and Chadwick had a sandwich and tea while Tracy had fruit and coffee and some cookies and they both talked about how much they loved each other while gazing into each others eyes, and wanted to spend the rest of their lives together and possibly have kids and be in love with each other for the rest of their lives, and as to how well they get along together and how much they both have

in common, and hope that
when the Cruise is over they will
get to spend even more time together,
they walked arm in arm up to a secluded area
where there was no one else around and Tracy told
Chadwick she had written a poem for him and asked to read
it and Chadwick responded "of course" as he took her tiny
soft hand and they looked deep into each other's eyes and she
began to read it in an almost crying raspy voice.

" when you love someone more than life,

You want to be with them all the time,

And I hope someday to be your wife,

I know deep inside you will always be mine,

I'll always want you day and night,

And I'll always be there for you,

And even though we sometimes fight,

I'll love you forever and always be true"

Chadwick told Tracy that this was the
most beautiful poem he had ever heard
and knowing that it was from

her heart made it more real
and Chadwick told her how he
was so lucky to have met her and he
believed that fate brought them together and
that it was meant to be and to have someone so nice
and so gorgeous in his life and how he hoped they would
someday marry, knowing he had to get rid of some skeletons
in the closet first then he put his arms around Tracy and they
embraced and he could feel her plump breast into his chest
as he pulled her even closer and could hear her groan and
whisper how much she loved him, "Make love to me again",
she said in a seductive partial whispering voice as she put her
wet tongue deep into Chadwick's open mouth and then his
ear and Chadwick said not right here and said someone might
come and catch us in the act and Tracy said she wanted him
now and she bent over lifting her skirt and pulling down her
silk panties and revealing her white rounded smooth butt as
it shined in the star light and Chadwick who was unable to
control his emotions opened his zipper and pulled out his
large throbbing manhood and rammed it up inside Tracy's
warm wet body and she screamed with pleasure and like a
raging bull, Chadwick made undying passionate love to
her until he exploded all over her back side and
as he heard Tracy moan and groan and say
under her breath how much she loved
Chadwick.

Afterwards they both left holding each other tight while walking through the decks of the large ship and gazing into the dark sea and then Chadwick walked her to her room and they hugged each other and they told each other how much they cared about each other and kissed good night.

Chadwick walked around the big ship for a while and went to the port side of the ship and leaned over the railing and while watching the white caps slapping the side of the ship, Chadwick started thinking about what a great time he and Tracy have been having on the ship and hoped it would never end knowing that he still had a secret needed to be resolved.

Chadwick walked into one of the cigar bars and and sat down, and ordered a rum drink and pulled out a cigar and cut off the end and lit it with a match and awhile later a man came in and sat on the bar stool beside him and he said his name was Nick and that he was from New Jersey, a small town near Philadelphia, Pa. and worked as a Postman there and was on his first cruise with his wife and her family of eight and Chadwick introduced himself and told the man he was having a great time on the cruise ship and also told him that he had met a nice young lady and

Nick said he was glad for him
and raised his glass for a toast to
all the happiness in the world and then
Chadwick shook hands with Nick and started
to walk back to his room and practiced some of the
Madam's meditations, and methods that she had told him
to do as much as possible and after meditating for about an
hour Chadwick laid back in his bed and started to pray, "if
there is a god please help me, and let me be normal and to be
able to Marry Tracy" whom he loved so very much and then
Chadwick went into the other room and got a glass of water,
and said good night to his mother and went to bed.

CHAPTER 19

September 19th 1955, at around 1 AM Tracy who was asleep in their room, found herself awake and she jumped out of bed and started howling so loudly it shook the room and like a mad dog she found herself partly busting out of her night clothes raving and panting and slobbering as her body was transforming from a beautiful young lady into a wild beast and she could feel her jaw stretching out of the normal and legs growing and getting covered with a thick gray long hair and her teeth were growing as her jaw was elongated out and with no control she was starting a rampage throughout the big ship as she moved freely place to place in a flash, first meeting a mate who was

cleaning in the hallway and
biting his head off and feasting
on him like a piranha in the Amazon
then she found herself going up the steps to
the main deck howling and taking out crew members
one after another and at one point she was confronted by
an armed guard and took him out after he shot at her and
she awoke other passengers whom she would kill with her
long claws coming from her elongated arms, she moved like
lighting throughout the ship and making her way to the
Captain's quarters and killing all deck hands along the way.
Once at the captain's room she knocked down the door and
entered and as she pounced toward him the captain had a
pistol and shot, hitting her in the right leg, but she continued
to kill him and tore up the blood soaked room and went to
the wheelhouse and killed everyone there and threw the main
ship wheel through the window and into the ocean and the
ship started to rock and turn onto its side as the rest of the
people screamed in the hallways,,,

Tracy then heard her mother's voice yelling out, "Tracy!
Tracy! Wake up" and she did, as she was having a nightmare
and telling Tracy that it must have been some dream,
after the nightmare Tracy now knew what could
happen if she did not take control of the
curse which inhabited her body,

her mother hugged her and gave her a glass of water and after thinking of Chadwick, she went back to sleep.

In the morning Tracy and her mother met with Chadwick and his mother at around 10am in the main dining room for breakfast, Tracy and her mother had coffee, scrambled eggs and toast while Chadwick had coffee, orange juice, toast and one fried egg sunny side down, and his mother just had coffee and donuts. They all started talking about how they will soon be going home and Tracy said she would be keeping in touch with Chadwick and hoped they would continue their relationship and Chadwick agreed as they finished their breakfast and Tracy told Chadwick that she had a nightmare after he left her room last night and slept, but did not go to any length as to what it was about. Chadwick and Tracy left the area to roam the big ship and left arm in arm, Tracy told Chadwick that there was another dance tonight after dinner and asked if he would like to take her, Chadwick said he would love to as they gazed into each other's eyes and kissed and they both explained how much they loved each other and wanted it to never end," both knowing that they have a problem that needs to be solved before that can happen", Tracy thinking "when do I tell him of the problem and will he understand", and Chadwick thinking the same thing as they continue to hold and kiss each other while standing by the rail overlooking the Ocean, after walking around for a while Chadwick walked Tracy back to her room and kissed her and then Chadwick walked back up to the Lido Deck to have a drink and think for a while, and while sitting at the bar he met a man by the name of Wang Fu who was on the ship with his wife and he told Chadwick that he worked for the US Federal Government as a scientist, Wang Fu was an interesting person and said he had been in the United States for about fifteen years and that his family ties dated all the way back to the Ming Dynasty and went on to say that he loved his job and working in America but could not tell Chadwick what kind of work that he did, but Chadwick got the impression that it was some type of top secret project and Wang Fu was very intelligent and Chadwick just being average person, mostly listened and after a while Chadwick shook hands with Wang Fu and left the area and went back his room, number I- 999 so he could rest awhile.

After resting in their rooms and at around 4 PM, Chadwick's mother woke him and told him that it was time to get dressed for dinner and Chadwick got up and took a bath

and shaved and put on his
blue suit with a white shirt and
a blue striped tie and black laced shoes
and his mother put on a long blue dress with
lace around the neckline and they started walking up
to the main dining room to have dinner and after entering
the main dining room, Chadwick seated his mother and they
ordered a steak cooked medium rare, blanched greens and
mashed potatoes and a bottle of red wine for their table and
then Tracy and her mother came in and Chadwick greeted
and seated them and Tracy was wearing a knee length skirt,
teal in color and her hair was up in a bun, and she was
wearing a white blouse that showed off her beautiful figure
very well," Chadwick was thinking of the dance and of
meeting Tracy afterwards and taking her to their special spot
on the smokestack deck" and they talked and ate and drank
wine and after dinner, Tracy and Chadwick left the beautiful
dining room arm in arm to go to the dance.

Once they arrived, Chadwick seated Tracy at one of the
tables and it was a big band with lots of brass and the band
was very good and Chadwick danced with Tracy to almost
every tune very closely and Tracy would sometimes put
her tongue into Chadwick's ear as he felt her
plump breast against his chest and they
were both in the own little utopia

and sometimes when the music would stop, they would still be on the dance floor in their own little world. Tracy and Chadwick left the dance at around 11 PM and walked arm in arm up to the SmokeStack Deck, and when they got there, they found they were all alone again with only each other. Tracy looked into Chadwick's eyes and pulled him close to her bosoms and told him how much she loved him, more than life itself and Chadwick said he loved her as much as he gazed into her starry eyes, and while nibbling on her neck and French kissing Tracy, Chadwick starting caressing her smooth thighs under her skirt and Tracy now had her tongue almost down Chadwick's throat and Chadwick felt her tongue tingling with his tongue while he was licking the roof of her mouth and Tracy laid down on the deck beside the SmokeStack deck and pulled Chadwick on top of her and said she wanted him to make passionate love to her so Chadwick put his hand up her skirt and felt the moistened wet place under her white panties while parting the hair with his fingers and Tracy moaned loudly and said she wanted to feel him inside her while grabbing Chadwick's behind and then Tracy undid Chadwick's pants and pulled out his throbbing manhood as she guided it into her wet body and Chadwick thrusting deep inside her as Tracy screamed with pleasure moaning and groaning as they rolled around while switching positions fingering and pawing and caressing each other's body like zoo animals that had just been released into the wild and made love like two thoroughbreds in-heat for about a half an hour and then afterwards holding each other for a while and composing themselves and hoping the night would never end, and they got up and walked away arm in arm while whispering into each other's ears as they walked, kissing from time to time as they looked at the stars and feeling the night air of the ocean night caps.

Chadwick walked Tracy back to her cabin and Chadwick then walked back to the main deck of the ship and found himself again at the bow of the ship, crying and thinking about all of the hunts that he had been on and all of the time he had wasted, knowing that he had to come to terms with the raging curse inside him and how he is learning to control the beast that is still trying to take over his body and knowing how much he loves someone for the first time in his life and doesn't want to fail in trying to live a normal life with the one he loves, "Tracy that's all that matters now," but when does he tell her about his problem and will she understand, he just wants to marry her and love her and have a normal life and possibly one day have kids and to have a house with a picket fence.

Chadwick started to remember about a year ago when he was walking out at night, in their neighborhood, he was only about six blocks from their house when he saw a young looking, blond haired lady who was sitting on her porch in a swing and when he got closer to her house, she spoke to him and Chadwick answered good evening as he continued to walk by the lady's house, Chadwick noticed that she was holding a kitten on her lap and she was stroking it and it had lots of fur and was dark in color and she asked Chadwick where he was going and Chadwick responded that he was just out for a walk, and then young lady invited him to come onto the porch and Chadwick came up to the porch and sat down beside her in the swing and in a frightening manner the kitten growled and jumped off her lap and ran away and she explained to Chadwick that her cat didn't like strangers.

They started conversing about each other's lives and she told Chadwick that she lived alone and later invited him in for coffee, she was wearing shorts, a T-shirt paired with sneakers, and once inside they sat on the couch and started watching TV and she then moved over and sat on

Chadwick's lap and went on
to say how lonely she had been
and they started to kiss and caress each
other and then she pulled Chadwick up off the
couch and led him into her bedroom. The walls were
pink in color and trimmed in white and there was a king
size bed pushed against the back wall of the room and she
then put on a record and dimmed the lights and went into
the bathroom and later came out wearing a see through white
nightgown and was carrying a leather braided bull whip in
her right hand and she handed the whip to Chadwick and
bent over and told him to whip her behind and Chadwick
gently struck her with the bull whip and she groaned and said
for him to hit her harder and Chadwick cracked the whip
hard and the young lady screamed and moaned. Afterwards
she grabbed Chadwick and started to kiss him and while he
was tasting her beautiful pink soft lips, Chadwick started to
undress and he started caressing her smooth legs, and the
rest of her tight body while pulling off her silk panties and
he then brought the young lady onto the king size bed and
Chadwick gently entered her body and made passionate love
to her in every position possible until they both reached the
height of orgasm and after about an hour of romping
in the bed, Chadwick was breathing hard,
his heart was beating fast and he was
drooling like a dog and could

feel his fangs coming out,
he pulled her head to one side
and entered her soft neck with his fangs
and she screamed and blood was squirting like
a severed femoral artery as the music on the record
player was playing and she screamed louder and then all went
quiet and her body went limp and like an out of control lion
feasting on a carcass in the jungle, he left her lifeless body on
the bed and left in a flash and went home.

After he stopped remembering, Chadwick now found
himself leaning over the ship's rail and with tears running
down his pale face, he cried out "why me", as he hated what
he had done in the past, but knowing how much he loves
Tracy, he believes that after one more session with the Madam
he hoped he will be able to control the rage that has been
haunting him since he was a teenager.

Chadwick composed himself and walked around for a
while longer before he went back to the cabin while thinking
about how much he loves Tracy and about how he hopes the
next meeting with Madam Medina will somehow remove
the curse of the vampire that's been controlling his life and
hopes that he and Tracy can get married and that he
can live a normal life and spend the rest of his
life as happy as he has been while on
the cruise and also knows that

he would make his mother
the happiest person in the world
knowing that he could live a normal
life and get married and at last knowing that
he was cured.

CHAPTER 20

September 20th 1955, Chadwick woke up and he and his mother got ready for breakfast and Chadwick told her that he had agreed to meet with Tracy and her mother on the Lido Deck at the buffet at around 10:30 AM.

Chadwick and his mother while walking up to the Lido Deck talked about him and Tracy and again Chadwick told his mother that he was in love with Tracy and was going to ask her to marry him tonight after his session with the Madam, but first he had to tell her why he was on the ship and he had had to tell Tracy that he was born half vampire because his dad was a full-fledged Vampire and he is tired of keeping it from her and she should know if they are to marry, and his mom agreed but stated that Tracy may not take it very well and not to be too surprised as to how she might respond.

Knowing that it would be a shocking revelation for anyone and she also noted that she hopes Chadwick and Tracy will be able to work it out since she seemed to be a very nice girl and they seemed so right for each other.

After reaching the Lido Deck Chadwick saw Tracy and her mother sitting at a table by the rail on the port side of the ship and they were eating pastries and drinking coffee. Chadwick and his mother went to the buffet and got their breakfast and a cup of hot coffee and went over to the table where Tracy and her mother was sitting and Chadwick and his mother spoke to both of them and commented as to what a nice morning it was and what looked to be the beginning of a nice day. Tracy was wearing a jumper type shorts that was green in color, sandals and Chadwick could not help but notice her brown tan long legs, which were crossed and her hair which was in a ponytail because she looked great and he told her that she looked nice and she thanked him and wanted to know if he wanted to go out by the pool at around 1 PM and Chadwick agreed to meet her there.

After brunch Chadwick hugged and kissed Tracy and then he and his mother went back to their room to rest and relax for a while and in the afternoon, Chadwick put on his swimming trunks and a T-shirt and headed up to the Lido Deck for a swim to meet with Tracy. When he arrived at the pool, Tracy was already there laying on one of the pool chairs on a towel and she looked great in a one piece bathing suit with a mini skirt built in and it was pink in color, showing off her beautiful figure and she asked him to come and sit down since she had saved him a pool chair beside her and Chadwick sat down and she sat up and turned around with her back to him and gave him a bottle of lotion and asked him to put it on her bare back and Chadwick put a little of the lotion on the palm of his hand and since he loved touching her soft skin, he started gently rubbing the lotion in a caressing manner and afterwards they both went into the pool for a swim since it was very humid.

They were hugging and holding hands while in the water and when no one was watching he would touch her under the water and they had a lot of fun and later they got out of the pool and dried each other off with a beach towel and then Chadwick and Tracy left the pool area and stopped by a bar at the end of the Lido Deck and they both had a rum drink and told each other how much they really cared about each other.

Chadwick walked Tracy back to her room and kissed and hugged her tightly and explained he would see her and her mother at dinner tonight but after dinner he would be spending some time with his mother, "knowing that he had to meet with Madam Medina after dinner", and Tracy said alright but she would miss him and maybe they could meet later on at around 11 PM at the smoke stack area and Chadwick agreed and left and went back to the cabin and laid down and rested for a while and at around 4 PM, Chadwick and his mother started getting ready for dinner, it was casually themed night so Chadwick put on his tan color pants and a green and white striped polo shirt and brown oxford shoes and his mother wore her sun flowered printed dress, and they walked up to the main dining room and after seating his mother, Tracy and her mother came in and Chadwick seated them both. Tracy was wearing a blue plaid skirt, knee length and a button up light blue blouse and had on pink lipstick with just enough blush and as usual she looked stunning and Chadwick commented to that effect and she thanked him. He and Tracy started talking and their

mothers were also conversing
as to what a great time they were
having on the big ship and they both
also noted that Chadwick and his mother
would be spending the evening together after dinner,
afterwards Chadwick and his mother left the dining area and
went back to their room and after about an hour Chadwick
left his mother in their room and went to see Madam Medina
and after arriving at the Madam's cabin, Chadwick knocked
on the partly opened door and the door came open by itself
and he heard a gruffly voice say "come on in Chadwick I've
been expecting you", and as Chadwick entered the room to
his amazement, sitting at the round table was the usual black
box in the middle and Tracy and the Madam said "do not be
alarmed", Tracy has also been seeing me and that is why she
too is on this ship, Tracy now knows of your problem and
now you will find out about her problem. She told Chadwick
that Tracy's father was a werewolf and her mother was not
and Tracy is half Werewolf and has been fighting the beast
inside her and hoped to be able to live a normal life just like
Chadwick has always been fighting the beast inside him,
Madam Medina had them hold hands and to look deep
into her eyes, and they did, as she chanted loudly
as green and purple smoke arose from the
black box on the table and she handed
them each a small glass which

had some type of blue colored liquid in them and both were told to hold hands and drink the potion and they embraced and drank the potion while the Madam loudly chanted and as she chanted again and again both were sweating as they gasped and fell onto the floor together still holding hands and Tracy coughed and a red spider about 2 inches came out of her mouth and at the same time Chadwick coughed a black toad about 3 inches in size came out of his mouth and the toad ate the spider and then the toad died and turned to ashes and the Madam swept the ashes into a little brown box and closed the lid and then Chadwick and Tracy both awoke and arose and the Madam asked how do you feel now and they both said great. The Madam gave the little brown box to Chadwick and told them both that on the 1st moonlit night to go to the north end of the ship and scatter the ashes in the ocean and throw the box overboard while holding hands and then the Madam said "my job is done here" and you can now go your way and live your lives and they both hugged the Madam and thanked her and left and walked up to the smokestack deck.

While walking arm in arm and kissing along the way, they arrived at the smokestack deck and found themselves all alone and they embraced and smiled at each other and were amazed to find out they had both been on the ship for the same reason and were very happy to know they were both cured.

Chadwick got down on one knee and put his right hand into Tracy's left hand and told her he loved her more than life itself and he asked her if she would be his bride and she cried and while in tears she said "yes, oh yes and that she loved him more than life," and believed it was meant to be that way and they embraced again and Chadwick pulled Tracy close to him as he put his right hand on her tight buttocks and caressed her breast with his other hand under her blouse and Tracy moaned and said with her soft voice that she wanted him to make passionate love to her now more than ever, and they made love for about thirty to forty minutes and they became one as he entered her beautiful smooth body and both of them reached the height of ecstasy.

After composing themselves Chadwick and Tracy both walked backed to his mother's cabin room 999 first and to explained to his mother as to what had transpired while with the Madam to explain that they were now both cured and could be married and he could finally live a normal life and together Chadwick and Tracy both left arm in arm as he walked her to her mother's room and once inside

she explained to her that
Chadwick was aboard the ship
for the same reason that she was and
that both of them had been seeing the Madam
and unbeknownst to either, they were being treated by
the Madam and was now set free from the curse that had
haunted them and while both were excited and smiling, they
told her mother as to what else had happened at the Madam's
room and Tracy's mother was crying with happiness and
hugged them both and hoped they would have a great life
together and Chadwick and Tracy then started making plans
for their wedding.

CHAPTER 21

September 21, 1955 The last day of the cruise, Chadwick was sleeping and was awakened by his mother, he jumped out of bed and said loudly, "this day is a great day and said he is very happy to be alive" and that he had slept better last night than any other time as far back as he can remember and when he went to sleep he dreamed about Tracy and him getting married and both now being able to live a normal life and knows she feels the same as he conversed with his mother with a big smile on his face and said this is the last night of the cruise and he wants it to be special for everyone. Chadwick thanked his mother for believing in him all of these years and for bringing him on this cruise and he kissed her on the cheek and hugged her and told her how much he loved her and told her she was the best mother in the whole world.

Chadwick started getting ready for brunch, "since it was now too late for breakfast," after bathing, Chadwick put on his tan pants and a green polo shirt and sneakers and his mother was already dressed and ready so they began to walk up to the Lido Deck and after they arrived they walked over to the food bar at the other end of the big ship, once there Chadwick got French toast, milk and coffee while his mother got scrambled eggs, juice and coffee. They walked over to sit down at a table near the rails on the starboard side of the ship and Chadwick saw a person that he had met earlier while roaming around the ship in one of the bars and his name was Bob Goodman and he was a Doctor in his forties and he was on vacation with his fiancé and her two kids. He was from Miami Florida and this was his third cruise but the first trip abroad and Bob spoke to Chadwick and Chadwick introduced him to his mother, Bob invited them both to sit with him and Chadwick seated his mother and pulled up another chair and sat down across from Bob while he and his mother conversed with Bob, Chadwick pulled out a Churchill size cigar and

cut the end off and pulled out
a match and lit it and Bob was
also smoking a cigar and was drinking
a glass of red wine and they all explained as to
what a great time they were all having on the cruise
ship and Chadwick began to tell Bob that he was engaged to
a young lady that he had met at the beginning of the cruise
and hoped to marry her as soon as they disembark and Bob
congratulated Chadwick and shook his hand and wished him
well and told Chadwick he was to get married at the end of
August and that he and his fiancé had been seeing each other
for about a year and he loved her and her kids very much and
Chadwick and his mother congratulated Bob and wished him
well and then Bob got up from the table and left the area and
afterwards Chadwick and his mother left the area as well and
continued to walk around the big ship.

At around one pm, Chadwick and his mother met with
Tracy and her mother in the main dining room for a late
lunch and as soon as they entered the room, Tracy who was
already seated got up from the table and ran to Chadwick
and hugged him and kissed him and said she had missed him
and Chadwick said he had missed her as much and then
Chadwick seated her and his mother and then
Chadwick ordered the soup of the day,
which was broccoli and buttered

toasted bread and coffee and a piece of German chocolate cake for dessert and his mother also ordered her meal and then Chadwick and Tracy started talking about where they could get married once the ship ported in Miami and noted that they wanted to live with Chadwick and his mother for a while or until they could get a house of their own and Tracy went on to say that she will have to transfer her class records to a nursing school in Chicago and be able to continue her education and would like to sometime in the future, find a house for her mother in Chicago.

After conversing for a while, Chadwick walked Tracy back to her room and then he went back to their room for some rest and relaxation knowing this was the last night on the cruise and knowing they would be dining and dancing later.

After about two hours of relaxing, Chadwick and his mother started getting ready for dinner and since it was the last night of the cruise, it was a black tie dinner so Chadwick put on his black tuxedo and black bow tie, and cumberbun and a white shirt with cufflinks, while his mother put on her red long gown with a split to the knee and she put her hair back in a bun and held it together with a gold tone comb and they looked

like they were ready for the
red carpet.

At around five PM they started walking
up the steps to the main dining room and once
inside, Chadwick seated his mother and sat down. In
about ten minutes, Tracy and her mother came in and
Chadwick stood up and greeted them both and after kissing
Tracy and complementing her and her mother as to how
nice they both looked, he seated them and sat across from
Tracy and then they all ordered their dinners and Chadwick
ordered a bottle of champagne and said since this is the last
night on the cruise they needed to celebrate to the good times
and after their meals were brought out, the server brought
out the champagne and slowly poured everyone a drink into
the crystal champagne glasses and Chadwick made a toast
to the great times they have had and the great times ahead
and everyone raised their glasses and sipped their drink and
Chadwick and Tracy talked about how much they cared
about each other and are glad things worked out for them
and that this was just the beginning as they drank their
Champagne.

After dinner, Chadwick and Tracy left the main
dining room to walk around the ship, and
they found themselves at the bow of the
ship on this calm, star lit night

and Chadwick looked deep into Tracy's eyes as he could see the reflection of the stars shining off of the ocean, and he told her that he loved her with all of his heart and wanted to be with her forever and hoped that one day she would bear his children and Tracy grabbed Chadwick and pulled his chest close to her plump breast, which Chadwick could feel through his shirt and jacket and they kissed passionately and heard a crewman coming so they decided to go to the dance, which was going on in the green room and after walking Tracy to the green room, Chadwick seated her at a table in the corner of the room and asked Tracy if she wanted to dance and Tracy said of course honey and they went onto the dance floor.

While dancing to a slow tune and Chadwick was holding Tracy very closely, the music stopped and they kept on dancing just like they were in their own little world and afterwards they ordered a drink and sat at the table holding hands looking into each other's eyes smiling most of the time and after a few more dances, Chadwick and Tracy headed down to their cabin room and Chadwick told Tracy that his mother was not there and would not be back for a while because she had went to another magic show with Tracy's mother and they had the room all to themselves.

Tracy was very happy and could not wait to get to the their room, Tracy was pulling on Chadwick and nibbling on his ear while they were walking and once inside the room they started hugging and kissing passionately, tasting each other with their tongues and once inside the room, Chadwick threw Tracy gently onto the bed and her blue skirt flew up revealing her pink panties and her smooth thighs and Chadwick took off his pants and shirt and started kissing and licking her knees and working his way up to her silk panties and licking her through her panties while Tracy was moaning and telling him in her soft voice, "please don't stop" and at the same time pulling his head deeper into her crotch and Chadwick put his fingers into her pink silk panties and ripped them partly off and was licking the wetness that was relieved between her legs and like a tom cat lapping up milk, he could not get enough of her sweet smelling body and Tracy screamed and begged Chadwick to make unending love to her.

She wanted to feel all of him inside her now and after Chadwick held off as long as he could stand it, he slowly entered Tracy's tight wanting wet body and Tracy wrapped her legs around Chadwick and pulled him even deeper inside her and they went at it like two rabbits in the wild until Chadwick exploded like a volcano inside of her only to hear Tracy scream and moan again and tell him in her panting breath, how much she loved him and hoped that he would never leave her and afterwards Chadwick held Tracy very closely and said that he would never leave her because he loved her more than life itself and after all that they have been threw together, how could he ever leave her, and when they someday have kids, Chadwick noted that his kids will never be without a father.

CHAPTER 22

September 22, 1955, once off of the cruise ship in Miami Florida, Chadwick and his mother checked into a hotel where Tracy and her mother was staying and they got a room on the same floor and Tracy and Chadwick started looking in the phone books to see if they could find a clergyman who was certified to marry them and they found a Clergyman by the name of Reverend Damon and his big white church was not far from where they were staying so he agreed to marry them on such short notice and they set the date for September 25th and Chadwick and Tracy went to the courthouse and picked up a marriage license and went shopping with Chadwick's

and Tracy's mother to get
Tracy a wedding Gown, and
afterwards they went to a jewelry store
nearby and Tracy picked out a 1.5 CT diamond
ring and band set and it was beautiful and fit her
finger perfectly and Chadwick picked out a plain gold band
size 13 for himself and they left the jewelry store and went to
a local Mexican restaurant and they all ordered chicken tacos
salsa and chips, and soft drinks.

They left the area and had the taxi drop their mothers
off at the hotel. Tracy and Chadwick went to the cinemas to
watch a movie, Chadwick put his arm around Tracy and told
her several times how much he loved her and after kissing
and hugging while watching part of the movie, Chadwick
and Tracy left the area.

September 25th, 1955, Chadwick was nervous knowing
that his wedding day was finally here and he got up early
and he and his mother ate an early breakfast in the hotel
dining room and then they went back to their room and
Chadwick started getting ready for the big day, knowing that
the wedding was to start at one pm so Chadwick put on his
black tuxedo and a white long sleeve cufflink shirt
and a black vest and a black bow tie and black
shining lace up shoes and his mother
put on a nice knee length dress

with a little bow in front and
she put her hair up in bun.

Once at the church, the Reverend ushered Chadwick into another room up near the altar and told him to stay there until he called for him and after being in the room for about 30 minutes, "that seemed to be forever", he heard a note play on the piano and a knock at the door, and the Reverend asked him to come out and stand in front of him and Chadwick did and then he heard the wedding march playing and looked around and saw the most beautiful woman in the world, in an all-white gown, and a veil, that covered part of Tracy's gorgeous face.

Once the Reverend pronounced them as man and wife, they kissed passionately.

Shortly after the wedding, Chadwick and Tracy checked into another hotel near the beach and after walking around on the beach in their bare feet, looking at the waves while hugging and kissing, they went back to the honeymoon suite at the hotel and made love off and on all that night and the next day Chadwick, his new wife and his mother flew back to Chicago.

On October 24, 1955, Now in Chicago, Tracy found out that she was pregnant possibly with twins and when she told Chadwick that she had just got back from the doctor's office and she had told him that she was pregnant and that it most likely occurred sometime while on the cruise. Tracy told Chadwick that it also most likely happened, while at the smokestack deck, Chadwick and Tracy was very happy and told their mothers who were already thinking of ways to spoil their grandchildren and then Tracy started thinking that if she had gotten pregnant before the curse was removed from her and Chadwick that maybe the kids could be vampires or werewolves or even a mixture of both and she explained it to Chadwick and Chadwick said he hoped that they would have two happy normal children, but at this point he did not know what they could do about it "knowing in the back of his mind that Tracy might be right". Would they be normal, or would they have to go through life like he and Tracy had to endure, or even worse if it turned out that they are a cross between vampire and a werewolf.

www.ingramcontent.com/pod-product-compliance
Lightning Source LLC
Chambersburg PA
CBHW061619100726
47898CB00002B/731